MONSTER
prick

KENDALL RYAN

Monster Prick

Copyright © 2015 Kendall Ryan

Cover design by Sara Eirew

Editing by Ellie of LoveNBooks, and Alexandra Fresch

About the Book

Over my dead body.

That's what I told Gracie when she informed me of her plan to pick some random guy she met online to get rid of her pesky virginity.

If anyone is touching her, it's going to be me.

I shouldn't even be considering it, but I can't get it out of my head: her, under me, begging me.

* * *

Arrogant. Cocky. Prick.

Those are the words I'd use to describe my older brother's dangerously handsome best friend.

When he learned of my plan to kick off my white cotton briefs, ditching my good-girl persona once and for all by losing my virginity to the first eligible bachelor I could find, he flipped out. Said over his dead body.

He says if anyone's going to do it, it's going to be him.

I hate that I'm even considering his offer.

But I am … I *sooo* am.

Ever since he suggested it, all I can think about is his cocky smile on those full lips as he's driving into me.

But if we cross that line … will I ever be able to go back?

Praise for Screwed

"Irresistibly sexy, witty and delightful." (Vilma's Book Blog)

"For fans of dirty mouths and dirtier deeds, Hayden Oliver is the man for you! Screwed is definitely a guilty pleasure read." (USA Today bestselling author R.S. Grey)

"Dirty and delicious -- I loved Screwed!" (New York Times and USA Today bestselling author Jennifer Probst)

"Kendall Ryan brings her talent for writing sexy men and steamy romance to her first (and hopefully not last) romantic comedy. Readers will be squirming and laughing as Hayden "The Playboy" Oliver attempts to be "just friends" with sassy, smart Emery Winters. He's so screwed." (USA Today bestselling author Daisy Prescott)

"Screwed is a hot, humorous, heady, and hypnotizing romance that sucks you in from the very first page-- consuming your heart, soul, and panties--you'll want to eat up this deliciously decadent book with lightning speed. Kendall Ryan's writing is refreshing and raw--a breath of fresh air--sprinkled with humor and heat." (Karen M, Bookalicious Babes Blog)

"Screwed is sexy, flirty, and funny as hell. Hayden and Emery's chemistry was amazing, pulling you in from the very first page as you find yourself lost in their story, not wanting it to end." (New York Times and USA Today bestselling author Kelly Elliott)

Chapter One

Gracie

I'm in a celebratory mood as I sip my third appletini and glance around at the sleek modern décor of the lounge. My brother, Hayden, invited me out for a congratulatory happy hour after I completed my first week as Peterson Design's newest architect. I was all too happy to accept. Free drinks at a posh club in downtown LA? Count me in.

I hadn't counted on the fact that Hudson Stone, his best friend and business partner—and my lifelong crush—would also be joining us. When he strolls in looking like a walking aphrodisiac, the temperature in the club seems to rise ten degrees and my underarms start to sweat. He's as tall, dark, and ruggedly handsome as ever. Despite the slight chill in the early fall air, he's dressed in jeans and a black short-sleeved T-shirt, which do nothing to hide his delicious muscles.

I panic for a moment about how I look, dressed

smartly in a jacket and slacks that were fine for the office, but not so much for an evening out. But the vodka coursing through my veins quickly takes care of that. And when he gets close, his cologne- and pheromone-laced scent delivers a powerful punch that knocks all other thoughts out of my mind. *Hello there, libido.* My pulse pounds in time with the low thumping music.

"Congratulations, Gracie. You're finally an adult now," Hudson says, leaning down to give me a one-armed hug where I sit perched on my barstool. My pussy squeezes a little at the tone of his warm, husky voice right in my ear. Did I mention I need to get laid? Like, yesterday?

"Something like that." I shrug off his compliment. At twenty-two years old, I've been an adult for a long damn time. It's frustrating that he's taken so long to see me that way. No matter how sexy his voice is when he says it...the prick.

Hudson slides onto the barstool next to mine. Within seconds, a bouncy-chested blonde waitress arrives to fulfill his order, and probably anything else he'd like, too.

His eyes watch her backside as she saunters away. It's then that I notice women throughout the club venturing hungry gazes over toward Hudson, openly admiring his chiseled arms and broad shoulders. He could easily have his pick of any woman here, and later, I'm sure he will. A fact I try not to dwell on.

"Cheers," my brother Hayden calls out. He raises his glass, pride beaming across his face.

"To Gracie." Hudson's eyes linger on mine for several intense moments. A warm shiver races through my body, my heartbeat thudding away. Seriously, they need to adjust the thermostat in this place.

Our moment ends when the eager waitress delivers Hudson's beer, lingering at our table even as we all ignore her. I look away and squelch my disappointment.

But when I glance up again, Hudson is still looking at me as he takes a sip from his frosty pint glass. I wonder what he sees when he looks at me after all these years.

When we met as kids, I was average in every way. I made good grades, but nothing that could ever qualify as "gifted," like my big sister Beth. She was the smart, studious one. She excelled in choir, too; we'd all pack into Mom's SUV and drive to see her in regional competitions. And Hayden was the athlete. I spent years of my life sitting in the bleachers with my parents, watching him run up and down the court with a ball. Sports were even less of my thing than academics. A friend talked me into joining track in eighth grade. I was excited at first. It was all so fun and different at practice: learning to conquer the hurdles, pumping my arms and legs as fast as I could for the fifty-meter sprints. But the time came when the coach assigned everyone to an event. I got the two-mile, the longest run in track and field. I hated it. And I was horrible at it. Huffing and puffing with a bright red face, struggling in dead last to the finish line where my inhaler was waiting for me. No thank you—that ended my illustrious track career.

I never quite found my place as I grew up either. I felt invisible inside my own family. But my saving grace was Hudson. He was always at our house, hanging out with my brother; he'd sneak into the back yard, where I often went to think, or duck into the kitchen to find me alone. He'd ask me about school and my friends and boys. He'd compliment me, and he never made me feel stupid. I felt safe around him. Someone I looked up to and admired was taking an interest in my life. It made me feel like I was worthwhile, and I grew to cherish our stolen moments together.

Once in a while, on an unpredictable schedule, Hudson would leave me a children's book under my pillow. Sometimes they appeared every couple of weeks; other times, months passed in between. But he never forgot. I loved to read, and I especially liked picture books. Long after I finally outgrew them, I still treasured each one he picked for me. They were never about princesses. They were all different, but they always had a message. Accepting your differences. Overcoming adversity. I think Hudson was the only one who noticed how I struggled to fit into my own family.

Then I got boobs and everything changed. They just kept getting bigger and bigger, until by eleventh grade, I was a full C-cup. On my small frame, they looked like I was smuggling grapefruits—big and bouncy and hard to hide. Hudson's eyes would zero in on my chest and he'd frown, looking frustrated. I would catch him watching me as I jumped on the trampoline in my parents' backyard. The kiddie books stopped then, along with his attention. He started spending less time with me and more time screwing anything that moved. He and my brother were disgusting. Through the bedroom wall we shared, I would overhear them talking about their latest conquests. They tag-teamed girls and compared notes. It was crushing to hear. Because I knew, despite all his attention, he'd never viewed me that way.

It felt like I lost the one person who really cared. And though I tried to move on, I still found myself getting jealous of the girls he fucked one after the other. Even on the days when I hated him, I wished that he would see me as a woman, not some annoying little kid. I couldn't help my teenage fantasies: Hudson pressing me into my bed, a cocky smile on those full lips as he drove into me with deep, powerful thrusts.

"Now that you've landed your dream job, what's next?" my brother asks, pulling me back into the present. He's grinning at me and I can practically feel the pride radiating from him. It makes me sit up a little taller in my seat.

It took me a few months to find my perfect job after I graduated from college last spring. Now I finally feel like I'm on the right path—and it's inspired some changes in my personal life, too.

"Funny you should ask." I place my elbows on the table, leaning forward like I'm about to let them in on a big secret. And maybe I am. "I've signed up on one of those online dating sites. I figure it's time to take life by the balls." I hiccup. "Excuse me. And now that I'm on the career path I've always dreamed of, my next step is to land a great guy, too." I've never really dated before, and I'm more than ready to get out there and start meeting people. More importantly, it's high time I lose my virginity. I've begun to feel like it's hanging over my head, following me around like a black cloud.

Well, that ends now. Because as pathetic as it was to graduate from high school still a virgin, lusting after something I could never have, it's ten thousand times worse to graduate from *college* still in the same stupid predicament. The main reason I'm still a virgin is because I held out hope for Hudson being my first, but I know it'll never happen. I need to finally let that dream die. This is the year that Gracie Oliver grows up. I'm nervous about it, but excited, too—it's just another way I'm taking charge of my life.

My brother's face falls, a deep line appearing between his brows. I look over to Hudson to back me up. But he growls out an expletive and his expression looks like I've just kicked his puppy.

Geez. What the fuck?

"For all those brains you have, that's a terrible fucking idea," Hayden groans. "You could meet a psycho serial killer, get dismembered and left in some dude's basement."

I glare at my idiot brother. "Women join online dating sites every day. It's not that risky, Hayden."

My gaze cuts over to Hudson again to see what his argument might be. He's tight-lipped and quiet, the clench of his ticking jaw his only movement.

"I just think you should concentrate on your career, Gracie. I don't want you to lose focus. I don't think dating is the best idea right now."

His tone is full of genuine concern, but I don't have the patience for his overprotective bullshit right now. Wasn't he just gushing about how proud he was of me for landing a job? I can pay my own rent, but not find my own boyfriend? "Hayden, you've never thought dating was a good idea," I snap. "That's why I'm a pathetic twenty-two-year-old virgin who's only just moved out of Mom and Dad's. It's time I grow up."

"That doesn't mean running out and doing something stupid."

Okay, fuck this. I'm not going to sit here and let him talk down to me like a little kid. Knowing that I'm fighting a losing battle, I slap down some money on the table and stand up, shaking with anger in my heels. "Goodnight," I mutter, grabbing my purse and storming from the table.

I exit the club and stop on the sidewalk. I consider taking a cab, then decide that a brisk walk home is exactly what I need to clear my head instead. Besides, my apartment isn't so far.

I tip my head back and look straight up at the darkening sky. God, the two of them together are the most macho, bull-headed assholes. Hayden takes the big-brother thing to the extreme, he always has. And Hudson used to be sweet, but these last few years, he's turned into a monster prick. He all but ignores me, and then when I suggest dating, he freaks out just as bad as Hayden.

Well, I'm not going to let them stop me. It's time I kicked off my white cotton briefs and had some fun.

"Gracie, wait," Hudson calls from somewhere behind me.

I turn around and stare into the most beautiful honey-colored eyes I've ever seen.

Chapter Two

Hudson

Gracie stomps out, heels clacking and chestnut hair swishing. Her face is cute even when it's set in a stubborn scowl. But I suspect she wouldn't appreciate that comment right now.

Maybe I should have stepped in. What could I say, though? As she argued with Hayden, it was all I could do to keep my cool. Just the idea of some random Craigslist schlub pawing at her...she hasn't even picked a guy yet, and I already want to punch him.

I shouldn't let my hormones take control like this. I thought I buried my feelings for Gracie a long time ago. We've known each other since we were both kids. When I became a man—and I realized she was becoming a woman—I did my best to shut things down. The only crime worse than messing with your best friend's lover is messing with his sister.

But I guess I haven't moved on as well as I

thought. My blood is still boiling at the thought of Gracie in another man's arms. Even if he isn't the least bit dangerous, even if he treats her like the princess she is...fuck no. Unacceptable.

I try to convince myself that I'm just protecting her. Just being a good big brother, like Hayden. He's flipping out about this too, right? I can be worried without it getting weird.

Deep down, though, I know I'm not worried. I'm pissed. A deep, primal kind of pissed. Territorial and jealous. I want to fight off every challenger...and bury myself in her until she screams that she's mine.

Shit, what am I going to do? I glance over at Hayden. He still looks thrown off, angry and skeeved out and a little lost. I can't really blame him. His precious baby sister is all grown up—*God, is she ever*—and she's just thrown that fact in his face. Nobody wants to think about their siblings rolling in the hay.

"Let me chase after her," I say. Now that I've had a chance to gather my thoughts, I want to talk to Gracie. And no woman, let alone one as pretty and tiny as Gracie, should walk alone in downtown LA after sunset.

"I'll make sure she gets home safe."

Hayden claps me on the shoulder. "Thanks, man. I'm sure she'll calm down eventually...but she probably doesn't want to see me right now."

"You just want me to save you from getting bitched out on the phone tomorrow."

He snorts a little chuckle. "What can I say? She's always liked you better."

Leaving my half-full beer on the counter, I dart out after Gracie.

Through the wandering crowd, all laughing and chatting and enjoying the autumn crispness, I spot Gracie a little ways up the street from the bar. There's only so fast she can hustle in those heels. Her hips pop from side to side as she speed-walks; my eyes fall to the cute, round ass encased in her tight work slacks. *Fuck me running.* Earlier, when I'd walked in to see her sitting at the bar with Hayden, I was taken aback by how professional she looked...and how sexy "professional" was on her. I guess anything can be a turn-on when

Gracie wears it.

"Gracie, wait," I call out.

She turns her face away from the night sky and back to me. "What," she replies flatly. But she stops, waiting for me to catch up with her, and I take that as a good sign.

"Sorry. I kind of...just sat there like a numb-nuts," I say. "Can we start over?"

"Not if you're trying to change my mind." Her full lips are still in a resolute pout. "I'm doing this. You and Hayden can't stop me."

I hold up a hand to show my defeat. "Okay, okay. I won't argue with you. But I am walking you home...it's getting dark."

She cocks her head, either judging the sincerity in my face or noticing the streetlights blinking on. Finally she nods. "Okay. I'll let you."

Does she know that my reasons for acting chivalrous aren't totally innocent? She elbows me as she walks by, a playful shove, and I resist the urge to tickle her like I did when she was ten. There's no way that putting my hands on her can end well.

* * *

As we walk to her apartment, we slowly start talking again, the bar blowup forgotten—or at least set aside. I ask her more about her new job. She jokes that I'll be investing in one of her designs someday; I tease back that I don't buy dingbats, and she sticks her tongue out at me. We reach her yellow adobe building all too soon.

Evidently she thinks so, too. Instead of going inside, she lingers on the stoop, fiddling with her keys almost shyly. "You want to come up for a little bit?"

Caught off guard, I ask, "Y-you're not tired?" What a dumb fucking question, Hudson. It's not even nine yet.

She shrugs with a slight smile. "The night kind of

got...cut short. We didn't get to finish our drinks."

She's acting almost sheepish. Does she feel like it's her fault that the party ended early? Even though it was her party in the first place and Hayden was the one acting like a tool. I know I shouldn't accept her invitation—she's still totally off limits, and there's no point in tempting myself with what I can't have. But I don't want to leave her hanging. And to be honest, I can't pass up the chance to spend time with her.

I give in and shrug. "Sure. One drink can't hurt."

Her smile goes big and bright. She scampers up the stairs, with me trailing after and trying not to stare up at her ass.

Her place is a small, cheerfully cluttered one-bedroom. I've seen enough properties to tell that this one was on the boring side when she first leased it; the furniture is sleek, modern, and lifeless. But Gracie has given everything her own unique touch. Gauzy curtains, jewel-toned throw pillows, a quirky zigzag floor lamp, a spider plant by the window, a seashell on the end table. The effect isn't little-girlish, but feminine and playful. A few Japanese ink paintings of flowers and mountains are squeezed onto the walls between the overflowing bookcases. And their highest shelves are all occupied with children's books that I recognize as my own gifts.

Did she put them up there because she wants to admire them, or because she doesn't read them often? Either way, she kept them all. And she went to the effort of moving them from her family home to her first adult apartment. I didn't know she'd done all that.

Gracie kicks off her shoes into the entry closet, drawing my attention back. I can see her much better in this light. Supermodel cheekbones and sapphire eyes, framed by tousled, wavy dark brown hair. A heart-shaped ass tapering down to legs that look miles long even without heels. Soft, full breasts nuzzling together under her white linen blouse. It hits me all over again that she's a woman. She's been a woman for a while, but now, she has her own career, her own place...and her own love life to prove it. I feel twin sparks of arousal and jealousy.

We get our drinks from the fridge—another beer for me, a wine cooler for her—and sit down on the couch. Even at the opposite end, I can catch whiffs of her peachy perfume. The walk home must have made her sweat. She sips her wine, red lips kissing the edge of her glass.

I swallow back the urge to touch her. Smell her, taste her...*stop it, Hudson.* I'm noticing everything about Gracie and I can't turn it off.

"Come closer," she coaxes. "I want to show you something." She pats the cushion right next to her.

I scoot over as casually as I can. My cock is already starting to twitch to attention, but I should at least try to keep acting normal.

Fortunately, my mind jumps right back out of the gutter when she opens her laptop on the coffee table. On the screen is the website for the online dating service she'd been talking about. And at the top right, there's a "23" hovering over her envelope icon. She has twenty-three new messages. Twenty-fucking-three.

I clench my jaw. Of course men would jump all over a piece of fresh meat, especially a beauty like Gracie. She'd be a textbook girl-next-door type if she weren't so striking. Gentle, sweet...and innocent. How many of these pricks are just aiming to take advantage of someone like that? How dare *anyone* touch her?

Oblivious to my growing rage, Gracie clicks around, opening two new tabs. Each shows the profile of a different man. They look ridiculously wholesome and bland, like stock photo models or athletes on cereal boxes. "These are some of the guys I've been talking to. See, this one likes writing poetry and training his dog. And this one volunteers at a soup kitchen...would a serial killer do that?"

She probably picked the most harmless-seeming guys on her list to show me. Not that that stops me from wanting to growl at them.

I shake my head—at myself more than her. I need to pull my shit together. She's just trying to ease my mind, make me stop worrying about her safety. There's no way for her to know that this is pissing me off all over again. "It's not that easy to tell," I say. "Somehow I don't think a psycho would list 'duct tape' and 'blood' under his hobbies."

"Somehow I don't think an evil person would love

animals and homeless people," Gracie fires back. She raises her eyebrows at me: *See, I can play this game, too.*

"Hitler was a vegetarian who cried when his dog died."

She gives me a weird look. "How do you know that? And why is everyone trying to keep me from living my life? For Christ's sake, I'm twenty-two. Are you going to stop me from getting on city buses next?"

I shift to sit facing her, willing to risk losing myself in her wide blue eyes. "No, Gracie. I just don't understand. Look...why do you want to do this? Really?"

Chapter Three

Gracie

I still can't believe I'm sitting here with Hudson Stone. In my little apartment on my hand-me-down couch. His large frame seems to take up more room than necessary in the space, masculinity radiating from him like a powerful cologne. Just being near him is an aphrodisiac. He's staring intently down at my computer screen and there's a tick in his jaw again.

Showing him these one-dimensional men on the dating site only heightens my awareness that none of them measure up to the man seated beside me. He's all I've ever wanted. He's smart, kind, driven, and intuitive—once I get him away from my ornery brother, that is. Picking up on my moods and doing his best to cheer me up seems like more than most men would do. Especially for their friend's kid sister. When he and my brother went off to college, I saw him less often. But he still found ways to make me feel like I mattered. He started leaving presents for me again on his visits home, as if he felt safer with some distance between us. A book under my pillow at Christmastime, another one for Easter.

But there were still the hard times. Like when he went to Mexico for spring break and I had to endure the dozens of photos on his social media pages, each with a blonde, busty sorority girl hanging off him like he was her own personal jungle gym. I hated seeing stuff like that. It was one thing to know they happened, but another to actually see the women I was sure he was sleeping with.

And then, of course, these last several years while I was in college and he and my brother were busy building their empire. I didn't see much of him then, either. Which was just as well—I threw myself into my studies, earning dual degrees in architecture and structural engineering. It left very little time for dating, and because of that, I never really outgrew my secret Hudson Stone fantasies. But now that he's here, in the flesh, those dreams feel so potent and dangerous.

"I just don't understand. Why do you want to do this? Really?" he asks, his voice tense.

Somehow I can't help opening up. Maybe it's the alcohol, maybe because it's been a long and stressful week of work as I got acquainted with my new professional life. But mostly it's the effect Hudson has on me. He's like a truth serum.

"Because I..." I look down at my hands. "I'm tired of being a virgin and I just want to meet someone and get it over with."

His hand slides under my jawline and he lifts my chin until my eyes are on his. What I see in those honey depths makes my breath catch in my throat.

"You were serious. What you said at the bar...you've never been with a man?" he asks, his voice tender.

Thankful for his sympathy, I shake my head. "No one."

He suddenly looks angry, like he wants to punch something, and I don't understand why. "How is that even possible?" he asks.

I shake my head again, mesmerized by his stare,

because I'm really not sure how to answer that. I spent too much time studying? Too much time lusting after him? Neither of those are good answers.

"Then you shouldn't just give it away to one of these random guys, Gracie. That's not what you deserve."

His hand remains at my jawline, his thumb lightly rubbing back and forth across my cheek. The rough pads of his calloused fingers on my skin feel amazing. I barely resist the temptation to lean into his touch.

"What do I deserve then, Hudson? Tell me." I'm not sure when we started whispering, but I realize we're both talking in hushed tones. Our faces hover just a few inches apart; I can feel the warmth of his breath on my lips. God, I wish he'd just kiss me.

"What if I could help you?" he suggests, his voice a strained whisper.

Stunned, I draw in a lungful of air. "What do you mean?"

Chapter Four

Hudson

"What if I could help you?"

I have no idea what the hell I was thinking. The words just leaped out of my mouth. Listening to Gracie talk about kicking off her granny panties and popping her cherry with some random Internet dick...I guess it drove me temporarily insane.

But there's no taking back the idea now. Gracie sucks in her breath, blinking wide-eyed. "What do you mean?" she asks.

What *do* I mean? Here I am, sitting next to the world's most beautiful girl—drowning in her eyes, her scent, the gentle puff of her breath on my mouth that begs me to close the distance. I know what I want, but I also know what will happen if I take it. My best friend will rip off my balls and feed them to me. And I'll probably deserve every second.

But sweet Jesus, I'm pretty sure Gracie wants this too, and that's enough to blow my better judgment to pieces. All I care about right now is making her feel better. In as many ways as possible. And if her slightly quickened breathing, blown pupils, and flushed cheeks are anything to go by...

As an experiment, I dart out the tip of my tongue to wet my lips. Her darkened eyes drop like a magnet yanked them. *Yeah, bingo.* Having a little black book as thick as the dictionary has its advantages. I know damn well how to tell when a woman wants me.

And it's become crystal clear that Gracie *needs* me, too. I've always been her friend, her confidant and cheerleader. This virginity thing is clearly weighing on her mind. I can't stand the thought of her feeling inadequate or ashamed about herself. And if she's half as horny for me as I am for her, this could add up to a lot of fun for the both of us.

"It's just a suggestion. Since you want to get more sexual experience, we could do something about it together." As calmly as I can, I cross one leg over another to hide my lap. The mere thought of being the first man inside her has me rock-hard. Images pour through my mind … Her lush hair fanned out over the pillow as I slip in. Her big blue eyes widening with surprise at how good my cock feels. Her perky tits bouncing and soft fuckable mouth falling open as I start pumping in earnest. I try not to groan aloud.

"I...um..." Gracie's eyes skitter around the room, always returning to me. Her cheeks are furiously red now. But she doesn't draw back even an inch. "H-how would that work, exactly?"

That's a lot closer to a green light than I thought I'd get. "Nothing complicated. We'd meet up at my place—say, three times—and I'd teach you what I know." Taking a chance, I add, "What makes you come best. How to please a man. Anything you want to learn."

Her breath hitches. Just the tiniest possible noise, but I can hear it, and it makes me ache. She chews her lip in an internal struggle. I can see interest flickering in her and I wonder again if she's as aroused as I am.

"They wouldn't be real dates, if that's what you're worried about. I'd just be...like a tutor." I resist the urge to make a pun about *showing you the ropes*. I have no intention of springing bondage on an inexperienced woman, but I don't want to push my luck and scare her off with some stupid joke.

She chuckles. "A sex tutor? I think the word for that is 'gigolo.'"

Hope sparks in me. If she's teasing me like usual, that means she's feeling comfortable. "Hey, I'd never charge money. I share my expertise for the benefit of the community," I protest, putting my hand on my chest as if I've been mortally wounded.

"Pro *bone-o*," she snorts.

I laugh out loud, and soon she's giggling behind her hand, too. But the sexual tension doesn't drain from the atmosphere—it just changes form, becoming playful instead of heavy and unspoken. Seeing her cute dimpled grin definitely doesn't help me get my boner under control.

"I'll have to think about it," she says finally, and my stomach leaps hot with anticipation. "But I'm not sure how to explain this...thing to people."

"You don't owe anyone an explanation. It could be our little secret. Nobody has to know." *Especially not your mother hen of a brother.*

She stares into her wine for a minute. "When would we start?"

"I'm free tomorrow night if you want." I know I sound eager, but damn it, I really am.

"No, I have dinner with Melanie on Saturdays." She pauses just long enough to make me wonder if she's finally shooting me down. "But I can do Sunday night."

I feel a wash of relief, followed by desire. Despite being pretty sure that she wanted me, I'd still run the risk of coming on too strong and freaking her out. But she agreed—and less than forty-eight hours from now, she'll be mine. Mine to hold and kiss and taste and feel. "Great. How's eight o'clock at my place?"

She opens her mouth...

Then hesitates and closes it, looking down into her wine. Guilt is written all over her face. "No. I'm sorry. I can't."

Crap...I screwed up after all. "What's wrong?" I ask.

"I can't do this to Hayden. I know he wouldn't like us messing around."

I rest my hand on her shoulder. "I know how you feel. Hayden's my best friend and my business partner. I'd be taking a huge risk, too." Bigger than hers, probably—Hayden would be a lot less hard on his baby sister than on the douchebag who deflowered her. And it would affect our jobs, not just our personal lives. But I'm not going to point that out right now. This moment is all about Gracie, not me.

She gives me a look of skepticism and concern. Not anxious, exactly, but needing to be convinced. I can't tell if she's still tempted or if that's just my wishful thinking. "If it's such a big risk, why are you willing to take it?"

"You let me worry about that." *Because my boner has hit the emergency override switch in my brain* definitely isn't the answer she wants to hear.

She sighs through her nose. "I'm still not sure how I feel about lying to him."

"It's not lying," I insist. "It's just not over-sharing. Do you text him every time you go to the bathroom?"

She wrinkles her nose. "Ew...too much information."

"Exactly. There are some things it's okay to not mention. Sex is your private business, so he doesn't need to know."

When she continues to sit silent, I finish my train of thought. "Listen, Gracie...this is your own life. You get to decide what to do with it. Don't worry about what Hayden thinks. He's a big boy and he's going to have to face the fact that you're a grown woman now. If he judges you for having sex, he's a shithead."

That gets a weak smile out of her. "And a hypocrite," she adds softly.

"I wasn't going to say it," I agree, shrugging. Hayden had his reasons for sleeping around—pretty similar to mine, in fact—but there's no denying how he acted before Emery inspired him to shape up.

I give Gracie's shoulder one last squeeze and let go.

"Just think about it, okay? No pressure. I won't be offended if you change your mind." Though I will jerk myself raw, imagining what might have been, before I try to get on with my life.

She chews her lip again, then answers, "Sure. I'll let you know."

I can't resist smiling at her as I stand up. "I should probably head out now. But one more thing…" I pause on the other side of the coffee table. "If we *are* doing this? Promise me you won't see any of those guys from the website until we're done."

"Why not?" Her brow is furrowed in a way that means she's just this side of annoyed.

"Because the whole point is to learn from someone you already know and trust," I say carefully. I can't let her know how ragingly jealous the alternative makes me feel. Not just because it would be too much for my pride, but because she'd start doubting my judgment. "Someone who can find your clitoris and isn't an axe murderer."

She rolls her eyes. "I'm telling you, these guys

aren't..."

"If we meet up three times and you're not feeling it, then you can try them. But give me a chance to work. Get all the lessons before you start trying to put them into practice."

"Yes, sir, Mister Stone," she chirps with a half-smile. It was meant to be a sarcastic retort, but I swallow hard. The image of her in a schoolgirl's uniform, roleplaying a "hot for teacher" scene with me, is way too much when I'm not allowed to touch her yet.

I wave goodbye and let myself out, already putting together a class syllabus in my mind. Three nights to grant my dream woman her deepest desires. *This is going to be good...provided she says yes.*

Chapter Five

Gracie

Melanie and I are seated at our favorite dinner spot—Tucchi's in downtown LA. It's a pizza restaurant with a big wood-burning oven in the center and little round tables topped with white votive candles. It's casual and cute. Every Saturday we meet for goat cheese and roasted red pepper pizza and copious amounts of local wine. Calories don't count while we're having gossip and girl talk.

"So what's new with you, babe?" Melanie asks. "You wear that skirt I lent you yet?"

I shake my head. "I haven't had a chance. All I've been doing this week is work." That tiny pink scrap definitely isn't appropriate for the office. Hell, I'd feel embarrassed to look at myself in the mirror with it on.

"So wear it at work. Who gives a shit?" she laughs.

"Easy for you to say," I reply, smiling despite myself. "Clients don't come to *my* job hoping to look like me." As a hair stylist, Melanie always sports the latest color and cut, plus fashion-forward clothes that I'm way too chicken to pull off. Customers flock to her chair for just a little touch of that beauty magic. And ever since we met as college roommates, she's always encouraged me to step outside my comfort zone into more mature, sexy territory.

Well, she might just get her wish for juicy news tonight. Because I seriously need some advice about Hudson.

Even as I sit here, sipping red wine and tearing chunks off my breadstick, I still can't believe his offer. My belly tenses just thinking about it. Hudson actually being my first. Hudson actually *wanting* to be my first.

Logically though, I know he doesn't feel that way about me. He's just trying to save me from the awkward experience of doing it with some stranger I met on the Internet. I guess this is just another way he's looking out for me. It's just so freaking strange, I can still barely wrap my head around it, even twenty-four hours later.

"What are you doing to that poor breadstick?"

Melanie chuckles, eyeing my plate.

I look down at the crumbled remnants on the plate and push it away. "I have something kind of crazy to tell you."

Her chin perks up in interest, her third slice of pizza forgotten. "Do tell."

"Well...you know how I registered on that dating site?"

She nods. She was totally on board with my plan—practically pushed me to do it, in fact.

"I mentioned it to my brother and Hudson, and they both kind of freaked out. Hudson insisted on walking me home, and I invited him in so we could talk a little more."

"What do you mean he freaked out? Did he pull that bossy prick shit with you again?" She huffs out a sigh.

"Kind of. I admitted to him that I wanted one of the guys I met online to be my first, and finally lose my virginity once and for all."

She rolls her eyes. "It's not his business who you sleep with, Gracie."

"It might be," I say, taking a sip of my wine to fortify myself. "He, um … offered to be my first."

Red wine comes spewing out of Melanie's nose and mouth before she covers her face, coughing loudly into her cloth napkin. The nearby customers glance over at us until she gets her coughing fit under control. "He what?!" she barks across the table at me.

I thought Melanie would be happy for me. Excited, even. She knows how I feel about him; I figured she'd squeal and help pick out my outfit and give me advice. I never thought she'd get pissed about his offer. I rush to explain more.

"After we talked for a while, he offered to help me out. He said my first time shouldn't be with a random guy, and that we could, um … you know." My cheeks flush with heat and I look down at the table. How will I have the courage to actually seduce a man if I can't even say the words? Maybe it is better if Hudson and I just get it over with. I'd die of mortification if I tried to seduce one of my online dates and he turned me down.

Melanie is shaking her head, her plucked eyebrows drawn together. "A guy doesn't just offer to *help you out* by taking your virginity. That's weird. Really freaking weird." She scratches her chin. "Unless he actually likes you, too. And even then..."

I shake my head firmly. "No, he doesn't, Mel. You and I both know that."

She nods, agreeing. Hudson had his chance with me. He's never acted on it. Never even given me a hint he was interested. It's time to stop believing in foolish possibilities.

"Well, I'm against it," Melanie says finally. "The whole thing is just begging to go wrong. Like...what would your brother say?"

Hot shame burns through me. Hayden could never find out. Not only would he be super mad at me, but his relationship with Hudson would become very difficult. And they aren't just best friends—they're business partners, managing almost twenty million dollars' worth of real estate together. I would not want to be the reason for breaking any of that up. All I can say is, "Uh …"

Melanie interrupts my floundering. "Exactly. And that's just the tip of the iceberg. Your feelings for Hudson have always run deeper than they should have. After sex—and you have to trust me on this one—women can feel more connected by the experience than men. Aren't you worried about falling even harder for him?"

For some reason, her sympathetic expression annoys the crap out of me. "It'd just be sex, Mel. I know that." But her comment has already seeped down inside me, exposing a worry that I didn't want to consider. I can't shake it off now. "Besides, I told him I had to think it over. I still haven't decided."

She nods. "*If* you do it, my advice is to be careful. Don't involve your heart. Remember it's just physical."

I nod back, like I have this all under control. But the truth is, now I'm even more confused and unsure about what to do.

"Come on, let's go get one more drink. There's a new club that just opened a few blocks over."

I open my mouth to refuse. These shoes aren't great for walking in, and Mel never stops at one drink. But I realize it's the practical, level-headed Gracie that's gotten me into this mess in the first place. I need to be a little more reckless. And there's no time like the present. "Sure. Sounds great." I plaster on a smile.

After a short walk to the club, Melanie tugs the front of her shirt down, showing off generous amounts of cleavage, and we're awarded with immediate entry. No waiting in line for us.

One drink turns into two and then three. I'm sweaty from dancing, but I'm having fun. I'm glad I loosened up and went with the flow for once. But the flow hasn't given me any answers. I'm still totally and utterly confused about what to do with Hudson's offer. If I say no, will things get weird between us? Will we still be friends? And if I say yes … I shudder with excitement and fear. I can't imagine the possibility of saying yes. I know it will change things between us, but my mind won't even let me explore that. Maybe it's because I know, deep down, that I'll chicken out and say no.

A group of guys buy us our next drink, and I hate that I'm immediately comparing them to Hudson. They don't hold a candle to his tall, muscular frame, his cocky smile, or his intelligent wit. I can't think of anything I want to say to them...and the short one is way too grabby for my tastes.

"I have to pee!" I call out to Mel, who's grinding with some tattooed guy on the dance floor. She gives me a wave and a nod, quietly dismissing me. She'll be getting lucky tonight. *That makes one of us*, I think, as I make my way through the crowd and toward the back hallway where the restrooms are located. Of course there's a line.

I stop beside the cinder block wall, my feet aching. There are about a dozen girls ahead of me. It's going to be awhile. As I wait, my mind wanders to Hudson. His strong, fit physique, his spicy scent … the way my heart pounded when he offered to *help* me.

Stop it, Gracie. I can't let my brain keep spinning on

and on about Hudson. I'm out tonight to have fun.

As I try to clear my head, I count the girls still in line … ugh. Seven more to go. Wanting to focus on anything other than my aching feet, I let my mind wander to my brother and his new girlfriend, Emery. I'm so happy that he's found someone. Emery and I are close in age, and I can't help but compare myself to her. Of course she's gorgeous, headstrong, and fun, but she also landed a great job immediately upon graduating. It took me six long months of applying, interviewing, and getting rejected before Peterson offered me a position. Emery's no slouch in the boyfriend department either. Even though she claimed she wasn't looking, it took her, what, all of six weeks living in LA to land a boyfriend who's crazy about her. And it's saying something that the man is Hayden. Other than his college girlfriend, which is ancient history, I've never seen him in a committed relationship.

I guess I have one half of the equation. At least I have a great job. And maybe if I said yes to Hudson … I'd be one step closer to moving forward with my romantic life, too. I roll my eyes at myself. Yeah, I doubt that a pity fuck from my brother's friend counts.

But beggars can't be choosers, right?

The skin on the back of my neck prickles. I can feel someone watching me. I spin around and am stunned to see Hudson standing right in front of me, his dark, hungry eyes on mine. How is he here, at the same club on the same night? Kismet, maybe?

"What are you doing here?" I blurt.

He raises one dark brow, still studying me intently. "The better question is, what are you?"

"Melanie and I …" I start, before realizing he didn't answer my question, I'm not sure what I'm about to say, and I don't owe him an explanation anyway. I snap my mouth closed, staring at him. Hudson looks incredible. I can't believe it was just last night that we sat huddled on my couch looking at those online profiles. He's dressed in a navy button-down shirt with the sleeves pushed up his muscular forearms and a pair of dark wash jeans. I can smell the traces of his rich cologne. Crisp notes of pine, along with something sultry and dark that I can't put my finger on. I want to lean in closer and inhale against his neck, feel the brush of his stubble along my cheek.

Hudson clears his throat, pulling me from my little fantasy. "Did you have a chance to think about my offer?"

"I still don't understand," I admit. "Why are you doing this?"

"What's there to understand?" He leans closer and I can smell a trace of whiskey on his breath. "My hard cock, your tight little virgin cunt. It'll be fun." He winks at me, his full lips tugging up in a smirk. *The prick.*

For a second I think he's teasing me, just like he did when we were kids. But then I recognize the telltale edge to his voice. He wants me. Even if he doesn't return my feelings, he really does want me. Suddenly I feel powerful and desirable in a way I haven't before.

"Kiss me first," I say. "To see if we have chemistry."

He brings his mouth close...then stops, his lips resting mere inches from mine. "You're going to be the end of me, you know that right?" he whispers. Before I can answer, his teeth graze my lower lip, and then he sucks it into his mouth, nibbling it lightly. It's so unexpectedly sexy that I groan into his mouth and clutch his shirt in my fingers. Sweeping his tongue against mine, Hudson takes control of the kiss. It's hot and powerful and way different than I've ever been kissed before. My inner muscles clench deliciously and I groan again when suddenly he pulls away.

"How's that for chemistry? Did I pass your test?" His tone drops from smugness into something deeper, something primal that tugs between my legs. "Are your little white panties soaked right now?"

The prick is absolutely correct. And I don't even try to deny it. I want to feel his lips on mine again. And again.

"My cock has been rock hard all fucking day. Ever since last night ..." he groans. "It's all I can think about." He dips his head again, inhaling against the side of my neck and making a small growl of frustration. The revelation is mind-blowing. Hearing Hudson admit what I do to him—hearing how much power I have over him—is nothing short of staggering. Confidence and arousal rush through me. Little ol' me, with one of LA's most desirable men dying to touch me. I almost can't believe it...but my body sure does, and it wants to answer his call.

"This wouldn't be just sex, Gracie," he says next, totally surprising me. My heart surges. Does he mean...?

But then he continues, "I'd eat your pussy until you begged me to stop. I'd teach you how to please a man. How to give a proper blow job."

My heart comes crashing back down to Earth. Not that his suggestions aren't hot as hell, but they're still "just sex" as far as I'm concerned, and I'm getting tired of him dodging my question. I give him a contemptuous smile. "How thoughtful of you." Taking a step closer, I look up into his dark eyes. "Why would you even want to do this? With a virgin, you'd have to go slow and do all the work. Besides, I'll probably suck at it."

He chuckles darkly. "You really have no fuckin' idea, do you?"

"About what?" I blink up at him. I seriously have no clue. And I hate that.

"How good you're going to feel around me, how

your tight little body is going to clench around me, milk my cock...trust me, it'll be fun for me. I can't wait to see how many times I'm going to make you come."

I draw a shuddering breath, feeling so shaky and overwhelmed that I want to collapse into him. Somehow my legs hold me upright. *Thank you, God.*

"Tomorrow night. Eight o'clock. My place," he whispers. With that, he turns and leaves.

I still haven't decided what I'm going to do, but as I watch the powerful muscles in his shoulders flex as he walks away, I want nothing more than to rush out after him, hear more of those dirty endearments on his lips, and feel his mouth on mine. I can't believe that kiss. It was passionate. Intense. Better than I could have imagined, better than my wildest teenage dreams—where Hudson always played the starring role. Maybe it's the alcohol, or that kiss, or the fact that when faced with men who weren't Hudson, I wanted nothing to do with them...but I think I may have my answer after all.

Shit. I don't know if tomorrow night will come too fast or too slow.

Chapter Six

Hudson

It's finally Sunday, and my first "date" with Gracie is in less than four hours. I feel like a nervous teenager again. Sweating in front of my prom date's front door, checking my breath for the hundredth time, barely daring to imagine where the evening might take us. It's a little ridiculous; I'm a grown-ass man with plenty of experience under my belt. I lost my virginity before I could even drive, and my bed has rarely been empty since. I shouldn't be sweating this at all.

But I've never had an evening with someone like Gracie—because there *is* no one like her. She's special to me, for so many reasons. I only distracted myself with all those other women in the first place because I couldn't have her. And she's handed me a huge gift; it's my responsibility to make sure her first time is as good as possible. There can be nothing commonplace about what we're doing tonight. In a way, I'm almost as new to this as she is.

At least Gracie's father won't answer the door with a service pistol tucked in his belt, unlike my actual senior prom date. *Her big brother, on the other hand...*

As best I can, I push away the thought of Hayden. But our friendship lingers in the back of my mind.

I quickly vacuum and dust my apartment, then head to the liquor store. I consider tequila for Sunrises, but I don't want either of us to get too drunk tonight, so I choose some wine from Sonoma Valley: White Zinfandel for her, Cabernet Sauvignon for me. I stick the white in the fridge, leave the red on the kitchen counter, and jump in the shower. I shave, brush my teeth, and pat on a little cologne. I decide on blue jeans and a short-sleeved polo, casual but not sloppy.

Finally there's nothing else to prepare. I even loaded up some chill-out music to play quietly in the background. So I settle onto the couch to kill time with a political thriller novel, the latest from my favorite author. I've been reading it every night before bed. Its plot is tense, its characters are intriguing, and I've got no hope in hell of concentrating on it right now. My eyes wander over the same page three times without absorbing a single word.

At the quick knock on my door, I gratefully drop the book on the coffee table and get up to answer.

Gracie is wearing a light blue sundress, its halter top cradling her breasts and her chestnut hair cascading in waves down her exposed back. Her apple-red toes peek out of flat beige sandals. She usually paints her nails some shade of pink or purple; maybe she wanted to look more grown-up for such a momentous occasion? If that was the case, mission fucking accomplished. She's always cute, but right now, she's beautiful. Breathtaking, if I'm being honest.

She offers me an adorable smile somewhere between excited and nervous. "Um...hey," she says. "Am I late?"

I shake my head. "No, you're right on time." I stand aside so she can step through and then lock the door. "You want something to drink? I've got a White Zin chilled and ready to go."

She laughs a little as she toes off her sandals. "God, yes. You know me too well."

And I'm about to get to know you even better. This is so damn awkward. Buying the booze was definitely a smart move. We'll both need some time to loosen up before we get down to business, or the mood will be all wrong.

I pour our wine and we sit on the couch, like we did at her place just two short nights ago. Gracie inclines her head towards the stereo system. "Is this song by Fistful Of Colors?"

"Yeah, actually. You have a good ear. I didn't know you were into electronic music." For the most part, I'm not either. But the downtempo stuff makes great background noise when I'm working, reading...or entertaining women.

Gracie shrugs. The tension is already starting to ease out of her face. "Melanie used to love it, so I heard some of those bands a lot in college. That and R&B."

We talk about music for maybe fifteen minutes. When she trails off for more than a couple seconds, I decide that's my cue to move things along. "So, tell me. What were you thinking of for tonight?" I ask bluntly. I have a few ideas in my back pocket, and I can run this show for her if she wants, but I'm curious about whether she had anything in mind.

She pauses, wineglass at her lips, and slowly puts it back down again. Her cheeks have turned pink. "Uh...I don't know. I mean...w-what do you mean?"

"What do you want to learn?" I set my own glass on the coffee table. "I guess I should ask what you've done before. No point in spending too much time on stuff you already know."

"I've, um..." She takes a deep breath and tries to quickly rattle off her list. "I've made out with a few guys before. Heavy petting with clothes on. Second base once or twice. But I've never touched a...penis, or let anyone touch me...down there. Or done anything naked."

I tamp down a tiny flare of jealousy. It only makes sense that she'd have at least a little experience—a girl who looks like Gracie would have no shortage of male attention. And this date will go smoother if she's not totally naïve. Why didn't she ever go further, though? Was nobody the right guy for her?

I decide to table that question for another time and focus on my task. "How about we just kiss for now?" I suggest. "Start simple and see where things go."

Cheeks fully red now, she nods at me. I lean in...and it begins.

Just like last night, her mouth feels amazing, so soft and lush. I can already taste the hot nectar of the sweet wine on her breath. I can only imagine how the rest of her will feel and taste.

I lick at her vanilla-glossed lips, asking for permission, and she opens up with a barely audible sigh. My groin heats up and my core muscles relax and tense at the same time—a familiar sensation for a familiar dance. This is what I know best. Why was I stressing out before? With Gracie, even a simple kiss is heady, more exciting than any other woman I've known, but I'm still in my element. And I have a job to do.

She's eager, that's for sure, but she doesn't quite have the finer points down. Her lips open and close against mine almost randomly. Her tongue darts in and out, not sure where to find the happy medium between "timid" and "forceful." I cup her chin and caress her tongue with mine, coaxing it into a slow, sensual dance instead of a game of hide-and-seek. I nip at her lower lip and hear her breath hitch. I teach her by example, and I'm pleased to find that she's a fast learner. In five minutes I'm rock-hard and she's almost panting.

I let my free hand fall to her heaving chest. I gently squeeze one perky tit through the dress, my cock twitching when the stiff peak of her nipple grazes my palm. She rewards me with a soft moan. Time to really get started. I reach around her neck for the halter top's tie and she immediately mumbles, "There's a hook under the bow." I smirk a little; she's clearly ready to get this show on the road, and I'm all too happy to oblige.

The top of the dress falls down to reveal her naked chest. I knew she wasn't wearing a bra, because of the halter top and the way her breast fit into my hand—but fuck, it's a whole different deal seeing them in front of me. Gracie Oliver's tits, at long last. All my teenage fantasies come to life. They're perfect, creamy firm mounds topped by a cherry nipple, and I'm powerless to do anything but lean down for a taste.

She gasps aloud when my mouth closes around one peak. I quickly learn what draws the best noises out of her, and soon, her hips quiver against my stomach with every lick and suck. With one arm behind her back, I pull her closer to straddle me. I rub the heel of my free hand over her clothed crotch; she makes a swallowed noise of helpless eagerness. Wow, she's sensitive. Or maybe just pent up. Well, I'll take good care of that.

Looking up at her face, I reach down to caress her slim, smooth calf. She nods and I slip my hand further under her skirt, pushing aside the folds of cloth. Her hips quiver again when I stroke her inner thigh; she gasps again, even louder and more throaty this time, when I rub through her panties. The cotton slides easily over her pussy, soaking wet, and I can feel her heat right through the fabric.

"Are you ready?" I ask. Her body definitely is, but if she's going to get cold feet, now would be the most likely time.

Instead of the shy nod I expected, she pants, "Yes. I want you inside me."

Fuck me running. What man could refuse that? Just the sound of Gracie's voice saying those words makes my cock throb. I stand up—as best I can with no blood left in my head—and take her hand, then lead her to the bedroom.

Not bothering to shut the door, I help her shimmy out of her dress. It pools on the floor and leaves her standing in only a pair of white cotton briefs. "Panties off," I say, already drinking in the view. She's a goddess. Her body is even more perfect than I'd imagined. Every detail from her firm C-cups to her soft flat stomach, from the gentle curve of her hips and cute butt to her long, shapely legs.

After a minute of my admiration, she fidgets a little. "H-hey, this isn't fair. I'm naked and you still have all your clothes on."

"We can do something about that. Undress me."

Her lips part slightly in surprise. Maybe arousal, too. "Guys like that?"

"Sure they do. It shows them how much you want them." Any idiot who's too insecure to let a hot girl undress him isn't a guy Gracie should bother with. And giving her control over this part of the process should help boost her confidence.

She only hesitates for a second, then stands on tiptoe to pull my shirt over my head. Then she unbuttons and unzips my jeans and lets them fall. Her eyes widen with amazement. She wasn't the only one who skipped a critical piece of underwear today.

"Jesus," she exclaims, "how is this thing supposed to fit inside me?"

"You'll stretch. And I'll go as slow as you want." *Even if it's sheer torture.* "Gracie..." I almost groan when she pets the head, curious about the slickness that has beaded there. "You want to learn how to jerk me off, baby?" The pet name slips out of nowhere.

This time her mouth drops further open. Like everything else, it's a good look for her. "W-what? I was just..." she stammers. Then her desire and boldness reassert themselves, and she nods with a resolute pout. "Sure. Teach me."

I arrange her fingers to grip my shaft. Her delicate hand looks almost obscene on the thick, reddened flesh. Closing my hand around hers, I move it up and down to show her the best way to pump without tiring her arm. It feels fucking incredible and her tits bounce lightly with each stroke. Remembering I'm supposed to be actually imparting some wisdom, not just getting my cock jacked, I take a deep breath and try to cool down. "See that little bridge of skin there, right under the head?" I point out. "It's called the frenulum. That and the tip are the most sensitive places."

Without any prompting, she adds a little flick to her motion that rubs over the spot with every stroke, sending sparks of heat straight through me. *Fuuuck.* Tension quickly starts building in my groin. Soon I have to grip her wrist to stop her.

"Let's leave the rest for next time," I say, a little unsteadily. It's good to let her practice, but if she keeps touching me like that, I'll have to take a break before the main event. And I don't want to make her wait a single second longer. She clearly has the handjob basics down anyway.

She blinks and then gives me a cheeky grin. "Next time...okay. You're the professor here." She sounds like she's looking forward to it as much as I am.

I take a condom packet from my bedside drawer, tear it open, and hold it up. "I'm sure you know what this is. The side with the lube on it and the reservoir tip sticking out is the side that goes outward. Now..." Holding out the condom, I let my voice drop a little lower. "I want to see you put it on me."

Cheeks crimson, she accepts the condom, looking back and forth between my face and my rock-hard cock. Finally she gets down on her knees. My cock twitches at the sight, at the thought of her sweet pink mouth on me.

Concentrating with a cute crease between her brows, she rolls the condom on correctly and I bend down to reward her with a quick kiss. "You're a natural. Lie down on the bed when you're ready."

I chuckle when she immediately jumps up. I was worried about her being a nervous virgin and psyching herself out of a good experience, but hardly any of her earlier shyness is left. Am I that good or is she just that horny? I decide I don't care. All that matters right now is giving her the time of her life.

I follow her onto the bed and prompt her let her legs fall open. She parts her knees, showing herself to me. Kneeling before her, I take a moment to inspect her pussy with care. She's shaved bare, and I part her plump lips and using the pad of my thumb, stroke her clit in little circles. A helpless whimper rises in her throat.

"You're nice and wet for me," I say, my voice coming out too hoarse. "And very pretty down here." She really is. Soft bubblegum pink dewy folds, a little swollen clit I want to suck on, and a tiny opening I can't wait to fit myself inside of. *Jesus. Is this really about to happen?*

Pushing one finger inside her slowly, Gracie goes quiet and still. Her wide eyes are locked on mine as I draw my finger slowly in and out. She's so tight and hot that her pussy sucks at my finger, greedily drawing me in up to my last knuckle. My cock twitches in jealously.

"Okay so far?" I breathe.

"Yeah," she whispers.

My finger is slick with her wet heat and I can't stop watching the way her tight opening looks taking me, parting for me. The scent of her – sweet feminine arousal – is almost too much for me to handle. I want to bury my face in her cunt and eat her for hours. But something tells me I should mind my manners and get on with the lesson instead of indulging in my own fantasies.

Deciding it's time to get on with the show, I bring her legs up to rest around my waist. As I press a deep kiss to her mouth, I guide myself toward her core. When my cock nestles right up against her hot folds, I stop. "Are you sure?" I ask, giving her one last chance to change her mind.

"Very," Gracie says, sliding her wet pussy over me as we continue to kiss, our mouths unable to stay apart for long.

As clouded as my brain is by arousal, I try to focus in on everything. The way her breathing hitches when I push forward the tiniest bit. The pulse I can feel rioting in her throat when I press my mouth there. The way her tight channel grips me as I rock forward again—deeper this time.

Gracie groans, her discomfort mixed with pleasure. I slow down, kissing her deeply as I let her body adjust to the brand new invasion.

Even slick and soft with arousal, she's still tight as hell. I slip in millimeter by millimeter, stopping whenever she stiffens or squeaks. When I feel her begin to relax and accept me, I thrust further in and bite back a groan. No one has ever felt this good before. Our moans mix in the pheromone-heavy air and our heartbeats slam together.

When I finally bottom out, I look up at her—she's panting, eyes heavy-lidded, skin damp with sweat—and ask, "You okay? Want to stay like this for a little while?"

Her heels dig into the small of my back. "Just...keep moving..."

Slowly I pull out, and then ease back in again. "You're doing so good, baby," I murmur into her silky hair. It smells like lavender shampoo. "I know you can take me. We'll do it together."

She rocks her hips sharply and I take my cue to speed up. She makes little needy noises that shoot straight to my cock. I shift my angle, looking for her G-spot, and know I've found it when she gives a loud, guttural moan. I pull her hips to meet mine with every thrust, showing her how much better it feels when she moves, too. She immediately catches on.

"Your pussy feels so good around me," I grunt.

Leaving one hand on her hip to guide her, I rub her clit with my thumb. She cries out again, ragged and desperate. Her beautiful sapphire eyes are wild with desire. Lost in them, I can't look away, can't do anything but push her higher into pleasure.

Her body tenses and shakes. Her nails dig into my back. Finally she cries, "Oh...oh, don't stop, *Hudson*..." Her pussy clamps down on my cock, pulsing with the waves of her orgasm. I groan and let myself fall over the edge with her.

Still inside her, I take a moment to catch my breath,

resting above her on my elbows. She cranes her neck to kiss me: chaste, unhurried, affectionate, so different from the desperate passion of a few minutes ago. I return her soft kisses, enjoying the calm after the storm.

Her giggle is a subtle hum against my lips. "I did it," she says. "Virginity no more."

"Shall I alert the media?" I chuckle, and get a little bite on the chin for my teasing.

Half of me is already planning how to make our next date even better. The other half is still savoring this moment with Gracie, enveloped in her warmth, her exhausted satisfaction. Face to face.

Chapter Seven

Gracie

"Can you hand me that stack of copies?" Brandon asks.

I limp over to the copy machine and grab the stack of papers, thrusting them into my coworker's hand before easing myself gently back down into the office chair.

"What's wrong with you? Hurt yourself over the weekend?" he asks, watching me carefully.

"What? No." *Shit. Was I being that obvious?* "It's just the heels I'm wearing today," I lie as coolly as I can. "I'm still breaking them in." At least that part is true.

I'm pleasantly sore between my thighs. Nothing a little Tylenol can't handle. But geez, how embarrassing. Crossing my legs, I concentrate on the pile of work in front of me, unable to keep a smile off my lips. I've been daydreaming about Hudson all morning and my brain feels like mush.

Focus, Gracie. I leaf through the design workbook for the commercial remodel we're working on. Brandon's the project leader, only a couple of years older than me; it gives me hope that with hard work and some luck on my side, I'll be running my own projects in a few years.

My phone vibrates in my pocket and my lips curl into a smile. Hudson spent all morning and half the night sending me sweet messages. I read them all about twenty times. The first one, sent only hours after I left his place, was to check on me and see how I was feeling. At the time, I was still floating on cloud nine and didn't even realize how sore I was. How my panties clung to my sensitive skin, or how my hips bore the markings of his fingertips.

I look down at a new text from him.

HUDSON: How's your day so far?

I chuckle to myself. Melanie was right about feeling a deeper connection to him after sex, but he also seems to be more connected to me, too. For all the years

Hudson's had my phone number for emergencies or whatever, he's never texted me. Now he can't seem to stop himself. Not that I'm complaining. I would've died of curiosity wondering what he was thinking about—specifically, whether or not he was still thinking of me after our night together.

GRACIE: I'm feeling okay. Last night was kind of crazy.

HUDSON: I had fun. His response arrives almost instantly.

I can't believe we actually did it. I actually crossed the big V-card off my to-do list...and with Hudson Stone. A silly smile forms on my lips.

Once definitely isn't enough. I want to do that again. I'm not sure what he'll think if I admit that I want to see him again so quickly. He said "three times" before...but now that he got what he wanted, is he done with me? He might refuse, but considering that I'm still on a happy buzz, I risk the letdown.

GRACIE: When can we meet up again?

I hold my breath, waiting to see what he'll write

back. Several minutes pass and my stomach sinks. *Shit.* Why did I have to push things too far? He offered to help me get rid of my virginity, not to become a regular occurrence in my life. Then my phone vibrates again and my heart jumps into my throat.

HUDSON: Sorry, I was talking to your brother.

The feeling of ice-water rushing through my veins reminds me of what a terrible idea this is. I should just cut my losses now and move on. Then he texts again.

HUDSON: Come over tonight.

My fingers can't type fast enough.

GRACIE: Okay. What time?

I peek up at Brandon, hoping he hasn't noticed my new smartphone addiction. His furrowed brow as he stares down at a rendering says no.

HUDSON: Any time after six. I can order in dinner.

Sex and a meal? My new favorite combination. With a smile on my lips, I get back to work, knowing my evening looks promising.

* * *

Knowing I had plans with Hudson tonight made the workday drag by incredibly slowly. Finally five o'clock rolls around, and I grab my purse and scurry to the exit. I want to go home first and freshen up before heading to his place. When I arrive at my apartment, I rush inside and fly through the small space like a crazed person. Brushing my teeth, and touching up my makeup so I look refreshed.

Now I'm waiting on his doorstep. As I bring my hand up to knock, terrified regret flashes through me. *What am I doing here?* Was Melanie right all along? Is this going to end in a terrible crash-and-burn scenario, where I'm just a heartbroken shell of my former self when it's all over?

When Hudson opens the door, I'm greeted by the smell of roasting chicken and my stomach growls, perking right up. The stale peanut butter and jelly I had for lunch was a long time ago. And the sight of Hudson with a dishtowel slung over one shoulder, wearing a plain gray T-shirt and jeans, is a very nice one. Oddly sexy and domestic at the same time, like he's welcoming me home.

"Hi," I offer, not sure why I'm suddenly feeling so shy.

Hudson's features soften as he gazes down at me. "Are you doing okay?"

"Yeah," I lie smoothly. Honestly, I'm freaking confused about what this is. I had sex with my brother's best friend, not even twenty-four hours ago, and now here I am again. I've never done anything remotely this crazy before. It has paranoid thoughts flying through my mind—like, what if my brother drives by and sees my car parked outside Hudson's place? I'd have no plausible explanation. And witnessing a murder is something I'd rather not do tonight.

"I hope you're hungry," he says, ushering me inside.

I follow him to the kitchen and my eyes widen. It's an absolute mess. Bits of onion and potato peel are peppered all over the counter. A huge pan of roasted potatoes and a whole chicken rests on top of the stove. A dish of green beans and a plate of warmed dinner rolls sit on the kitchen island.

"Did your refrigerator explode?" I giggle.

He chuckles back. "I guess I was hungry. And I didn't feel like ordering takeout."

I step closer, surveying his work. *Wow. He did all this for me?* The chicken smells incredible and the potatoes are perfectly cooked, with little crispy edges just like I like. "I didn't know you knew how to cook."

He shrugs. "One of the benefits of being raised with a housekeeper who made us a big family dinner every night. I guess all those years doing my homework at the kitchen island while Greta cooked rubbed off on me."

I knew Hudson's family had money, but I guess I never paused to consider how different his upbringing was from mine. He opted to spend most of his free time over at our house, which is weird given that his parents' place boasted a pool, tennis court, and an in-home theater.

"Do you want to set the table while I finish up?"

I nod and he hands me two heavy porcelain plates. When he invited me over, I assumed we'd eat pizza off paper plates in front of the TV before heading into the bedroom. A home-cooked meal, served on real china, eaten while I cast nervous glances over at him from across the table...it feels a lot more serious. *Intimate.* I kind of like that, but it also bothers me, and I'm not sure why. Maybe because he'd said this was going to be just sex—strictly educational, nothing more—but this already feels like *more.* Ignoring the tightening in my belly, I dutifully take the plates and the silverware and set them on his dining table, where two glasses of ice water are sweating rings into the dark wood.

"I hope this is okay." Hudson joins me at the table, placing the chicken and side dishes in the center. "Help yourself."

I dig in, helping myself to a good portion of everything he's prepared. Hudson does the same, but I can't help but notice he keeps glancing in my direction.

After a few bites, which are delicious, I work up the courage to ask him about the elephant in the room. One of them, anyway. "So...you said you talked to my brother." Might as well get it out in the open. Besides, I don't think I'll be able to concentrate on anything else until we discuss it.

Hudson sets his fork down beside his plate and wipes his mouth with the napkin. "Yes. We had a meeting earlier about one of our buildings."

"How did that go?" I want to know if he was nervous, if he felt guilty, but his impassive expression and nonchalant tone make him very hard to read. Then again, he was always the type to hold his cards close to his chest, never overreacting or stirring up drama. It's probably what makes him so good at business. He's level-headed and calm.

He shrugs. "Don't worry, Gracie. He doesn't suspect anything."

My stomach twists again.

"We don't have to do anything you don't want to,"

he adds, his tone turning somber.

"I know," I squeak out. That's the thing, I do want to. I'm just worried about what happens when all of this inevitably comes to a crashing end.

"Will you tell me more about your job? I never got to hear the details, since your happy hour was cut short. Do you like the firm?" He leans forward, placing his elbows on the table.

I almost sag in relief, thankful for the change in topic. "Actually, I love it," I say, surprised at the sincerity in my voice. While I haven't exactly adjusted to waking up at six every morning and fighting traffic on my commute like a Real Grownup, I love my job. I fill him in on the details of my team's current project, a downtown renovation of a whole city block. Instead of his eyes glossing over with boredom, he nods with interest and asks insightful questions.

It's crazy how normal this all feels. Sharing a meal and conversation with him feels natural and casual just like always, only now I know how good he is in bed. I almost giggle to myself. *Almost*. But then Hudson is sharing his plans for next year, which includes purchasing a commercial space downtown for his and Hayden's new office, and he wants to get my perspective. I'm flattered and tell him of course I'll help.

Somehow we've been sitting here talking for almost two hours, the leftover food on our plates cold and forgotten. But then his eyes darken, a slow smile smoldering on his lips, and the atmosphere instantly changes. Electricity sparks between us, leaving the air hot and charged in its wake.

In a low, husky tone, Hudson asks, "Did you get enough to eat?"

A warm shiver races through me, knowing that the evening is about to take a turn. "Yes, thank you," I reply with a nod. I never knew he was such a great cook. Just another thing on the long list of things I admire about him. Melanie's warning about not falling for him flashes through my mind. I'm about to make some excuse, tell him I have to leave, when he rises from the table and stalks toward me.

"I've been going crazy all day, remembering the way you looked naked in my bed ..." He lifts me from my chair and my body immediately molds to his. Soft and pliable. His fingertips brush stray strands of hair back from my face.

"I can't stop thinking about how your body felt clenched around mine. You were perfection," he growls, bringing his mouth to my neck.

Forget a warm shiver—his words crack through me like a lightning strike, nearly splitting me in two. I've never felt so sexy or desired. It's only Hudson that makes me feel this way. The feeling has become addictive already.

"Hudson," I groan, lifting my lips to his. We kiss, passionately, like there's a fire chasing us. Pressing my hips closer, I can feel every hard inch of his arousal. My panties are already soaked. "Should we go to your bedroom?" I pant, breaking my mouth from his after several hot minutes.

"Whatever you want," he murmurs, nibbling my collarbone.

Whether he's giving me an opening to leave, or just implying that we can have our adventure somewhere other than the bed, I'm not sure. I definitely want to do this. But I'm not sure if I'm bold enough yet to move onto kitchen-counter sex or living-room-with-the-lights-on sex.

"Yes," is all I can say, but Hudson interprets it perfectly. He lifts me up and I wrap my legs around his waist as he carries me down the hallway toward his bedroom.

When my feet touch the floor, he immediately goes to work on the button of my dress pants. "Get naked," he whispers. His naughty voice commanding me in the darkness sends hot arousal zipping through my veins. I give my hips a wiggle as he pushes my pants and panties down over my butt.

"Sexy little thing," Hudson whispers, treating me to a quick kiss on the lips.

I never knew sex would be fun. It might sound weird, but I always assumed there would be a lot to concentrate on, with inserting tab A into slot B and whatnot. I'm relieved to see it's nothing like that. It's easy and natural.

I open my blouse, fumbling over the buttons as Hudson brings the back of his hand between my thighs and gently rubs his knuckles over my bare pussy. I press my thighs together as tingles shoot up my spine.

When I'm finally free of the shirt, Hudson unclasps my bra for me and his mouth lowers, taking one pert nipple into his mouth. The sensation makes me flinch it feels so good.

"Prettiest set of tits I've ever seen," he murmurs, moving to my other breast while he holds the weight of them in his hands. "I should fuck these before we're done. Would you like that, Gracie?"

A sobbing gasp gets stuck in my throat. *Done.* The word echoes in my head. I can't let myself think about the end of my time with him, or I'll start crying. Tears are already threatening to appear, even as good as his mouth and hands feel on me.

"On the bed," he pants, breaking away from my nipple with a groan that sends goosebumps racing along my skin.

I sit down on the edge of the bed and scoot up

toward the pillows. Then I watch, barely breathing, as Hudson treats me to an erotic strip show. He pulls his T-shirt off over his head that way guys do before dropping it to the floor, all of the hard muscles in his stomach and chest flexing as he moves. His deft fingers move to the button on his jeans, and then they're sliding down his powerful thighs along with his boxers. He is beautiful like this. He's hard edges and muscle, but this is him opening himself up to me, taking a risk, and making a huge jump with me off to crazy-horny town.

I reach out toward him and he joins me on the bed, his mouth moving to my breasts again while my right hand ventures down until I find the weight of his cock. I push my hand up and down just like he showed me, loving the heat of him and the little grunts he makes.

"Shit, Gracie, where did you learn to jack my cock like that?" He smirks at me.

"You." I grin right back at him.

Chuckling darkly, he moves down on the bed until he's eye-level with my navel. I inhale sharply when he kisses my belly. Then he moves lower and I forget how to breathe.

"I'm going to fuck this tight pussy until you beg me to stop," he pants, his teeth grazing my inner thigh.

His mouth closes over my clit and I cry out. His large hands hold my thighs open nice and wide and I take every bit of pleasure he doles out. His tongue moves in an expert pattern designed to bring me more pleasure than I could have dreamed possible. Then he pushes two fingers inside me and I groan, flinching as my back arches off the bed.

"Are you sore?" he asks, blinking up at me and my dramatic reaction.

I give a careful nod. I am a little sore, but not uncomfortable enough that I don't want to do this.

"Fuck." He sits back on his heels, his huge cock sticking straight up in the air. He scrubs a hand through his hair. "I didn't even think about that. It's been a long time since I was with a virgin. Forgive me?" he asks, tilting my chin up until I meet his dark, stormy eyes.

"Of course. It's nothing. I promise I'm okay." I won't tell him that I took pain reliever earlier, knowing that won't help the concerned look in his eyes.

His eyes search mine, and eventually, he decides to believe me. His mouth goes back to my core again. But this time he's softer, moving with the skill of a man who both knows what he's doing and doesn't want to push me too far.

Soon I'm clawing at the sheets, tugging at his hair, and rocking my hips into his mouth, not caring one little bit that I'm riding his face like a maniac. This only makes him more determined, and his tongue moves earnestly against me, drawing tight circles over my sensitive bud.

"Hudson," I cry out, my body convulsing once, twice, as a powerful orgasm washes over me. He crawls up my body and kisses me through every little aftershock.

"Feel good, princess?" he whispers in the darkness, his lips brushing mine.

"Very. Thank you."

"You don't have to thank me for doing that. Trust

me, it was my pleasure."

As strange as it is, I believe him. The look of reverence painted on his face tells me he enjoyed that almost as much as I did.

I pull him closer and lay back on the bed, parting my thighs.

"Are you sure?" he asks, his breath a whisper on my neck.

I nod tightly. "Positive." The way he pumped in and out of me last night while his thumb stroked my clit has played through my brain all day.

He grabs a condom from beside his bed and quickly slips it on. Then he's back, moving between my legs, looking into my eyes as he pushes forward. The broad tip of him pierces me and I groan, shifting my hips closer, wanting more of him.

"I want you to watch," he says, withdrawing just a bit. I look down to where our bodies are joined, and *damn*. That's an erotic sight. His thick cock is painted in my wetness, and my inner folds are parted to accept him. He thrusts in slow, but deep, until he grinds his pelvis against my clit. The tight bud is peeking out from its sheath and when he grinds against me, I shudder.

"Shit, *Hudson*," I moan out the curse, my eyes drifting closed.

"Watch, baby. Look how your pussy hugs me." He rocks against me, sliding in and out inch by delicious inch. His movements are slower, more controlled than last night. Is he less eager, or does he just want to savor this?

"Does it feel good for you, too?" I ask, noticing the tick in his hard-set jaw.

"Too good," he growls.

I know exactly what he means. My body is already building toward release, and I cry out with each deep thrust forward. Hudson joins me, a deep grunt rumbling in his chest as his pace picks up.

I push my hips up, meeting each of his hard thrusts as I drift closer and closer to the edge. Then he brings his thumb to my clit again and rubs it in small circles. Almost immediately my inner muscles clamp down around him and I cry out his name. A powerful orgasm races through my system, making me almost dizzy with the force of it. A thin sheen of sweat covers my body and my nipples are pebbled into hardened points. But Hudson's not done with me yet. He begins rocking into me in fast, uneven strokes as the aftershocks of my second orgasm continue to pulse quietly through me.

"*Gracie* ..." My name on his lips as he comes causes my pussy to flutter around him again. "Fucking hell, baby. You have no idea how good that felt," he says, pulling me into his arms. He collapses down onto the bed, holding me close. I rest my head on his chest and listen to the whooshing sound of his racing heart, wondering what in the hell just happened. It was almost better than our first time, if that's even possible; it must be because now he knows my body intimately and I know his. The thought makes me happy. But even as I close my eyes and try to relax, the gnawing anxiety I felt earlier refuses to fade completely.

* * *

Later that night, we're still relaxing together in his bed in post-sex bliss when Hudson suddenly sits up. "I have an idea …"

I think he's about to propose a crazy new sexual act that he wants to introduce me to. Rising to his feet, he offers me his hand, and I accept, standing naked before him. But then he completely surprises me.

"You feel like going to Sebastian's to get an ice cream?"

"You're inviting me for dessert?" I can't help the silly grin spreading over my face. We used to go to Sebastian's all the time when we were younger, but I haven't been in years.

"Why not?" He smiles and I'm lost.

"Of course I'll go."

We throw on our clothes and head out into the night. His hand rests on my knee while he drives, the radio playing low in the background. I'm happy to see the conversation flows just as well when our clothes are on. Then again, I always knew it would. I've known him since I was four years old and I've liked him almost that long. If I'm being honest, I've always felt a lot more for him than *like*.

But I force those thoughts away as we park outside one of the most popular independently owned ice cream shops in town. In the summer, this place has a line wrapping around the side of the building and down a whole city block. But given that it's early fall and we're here a little later in the evening, after the family crowd, there are only a few people ahead of us. Once inside, I stuff my hands in my pockets, feeling light and carefree as I gaze down into the glass-covered counter full of creamy delicacies. I'm already imagining how the sweet and savory pistachio ice cream will taste melting on my tongue when I hear a familiar laugh.

My whole body tenses up, breaking out in a cold sweat. My brother and Emery have just entered the shop. And when I glance over, Hayden's eyes lock with mine.

"Gracie?" With a lopsided smile, he starts to come closer, apparently forgetting about the line.

I'm in a full-on panic. There's no way to explain my

being here with Hudson. He and I are not friends—we do not grab ice cream together. And since I'm rocking the world's most obvious case of just-fucked hair, I'm pretty sure I'm busted. My heart slams against my ribs as I glance over to Hudson, praying that he'll step in and say just the right thing to rescue me.

Except he's not there. He's gone..

One second he was standing right beside me, providing a running commentary on his favorite flavor combinations. The next second, he's gone. *Poof. Vanished.*

"What are you doing here?" my brother asks, pulling me into a one-armed hug. Sebastian's is a good hike from my place, but it's right down the street from Hudson's. I hope to God he doesn't connect the dots.

I shrug, trying to act casual when inside I feel anything but. *Where the hell did Hudson go? Why'd he have to leave me to handle this myself?* "I was in the mood for some ice cream." *And some dick*, I mentally add.

"Cool. You can join us. We just finished dinner."

He gestures toward Emery, who's dutifully waiting in line. Must be nice to have a partner who sticks around to save your spot...and your ass.

"No, that's okay. I'm going to get going and leave you two to finish your date without a third wheel." He hasn't asked about Hudson yet, so he must have escaped before my brother could see him. Now I just have to make a break for it myself.

Hayden studies me quietly for a moment. "Are you okay? You look a little flushed." He raises a hand to my forehead, but I quickly brush him away.

"I'm fine. Excuse me," I say, noticing that I'm next in line and the cashier is looking more than a little annoyed. I order the first thing my eye lands on—one scoop of cherry bliss—and take my cup to go, waving at Emery and Hayden as I speed-walk outside.

The sidewalk is empty and I'm seriously not sure what happened to Hudson. Maybe he freaked out and went home. A pang of hurt ripples through me; I'm already starting to regret what I've done. Spooning a mouthful of ice cream into my mouth, I comfort myself with fat and sugar as I begin walking toward home.

Strong hands reach out and grab me, pushing me back against the brick building. I stiffen in shock and my mouth drops open to protest...only to be covered by firm lips kissing me in earnest. *Hudson.*

"Mmm, you taste like cherries." His tongue strokes mine, deepening the kiss as I groan against him. I want to yell at him for disappearing, but his warm mouth is on mine, his tongue coaxing mine to play. Besides, his disappearing act is the only reason we didn't get caught.

"My brother's right inside." I tip my head toward the front door, which is less than ten feet away.

Hudson grinds his erection against my hip and my insides go molten. I'm wondering if he's going to invite me back to his place for a second round when he suddenly pulls away. "Then we better get you in a cab. You have to work tomorrow."

I'm about to argue that he does too. But his expression is serious rather than playful, so I simply nod. This isn't a fluffy romantic movie. He isn't going to suddenly declare his love for me and storm inside to ask my brother for his blessing. He got what he wanted—

we fucked like rabbits earlier—and now he's ready to head home. Alone.

Moments later, I'm sitting in the back of a cab with a melting cup of ice cream, wondering what in the actual fuck I'm going to do when Hudson's done with me.

Chapter Eight

Hudson

I'd nearly forgotten about my basketball game with Hayden today. We always go to the gym after work on Tuesdays and Thursdays, but Gracie has crowded everything else out of my mind. At least, that's my excuse for why Hayden handed me my ass today. Not that I can tell him so.

"Dude, where did your game go to die?" Hayden laughs as we get changed in the locker room after. He's been nice enough to remind me—several times—about how many matches I just lost. "What's with you lately?"

"Right now, it's the fact that you won't put your fucking pants on," I reply. While I got dressed right away, he dawdled after his shower to keep making fun of me. There's several other men ambling around the locker room in their towels, but Hayden is the only one who's hovering near my bench seat, and I'd rather not deal with his crotch in my face anymore.

His kid sister, on the other hand... My mind conjures the image of Gracie wrapped in a towel, cheeks flushed from the hot water and hair clinging to her bare shoulders in dark tendrils. Just one flimsy layer of cloth separating me from her lithe body. I'd wrap my arms around her hips to pull her close, squeezing her firm, round ass, and the towel would slither to the floor. Then I'd work my tongue into her sweet...

I slam the brakes on that train of thought. A gym locker room is the absolute last place I want to get a boner. But making myself stop thinking about Gracie is easier said than done. In just a few days, she's worked her way under my skin.

"Seriously, man. I've hardly heard from you since we had drinks with Gracie last Friday. You bailed on that new club we were going to check out. Yesterday, I emailed you about Windsor Heights and you replied about Washington Gardens." He gives me a sly look. "You find a new booty call or something?"

I almost knock my bag onto the gross wet floor. "The hell are you smoking?" I scoff, hoping I sound incredulous rather than caught red-handed. Gracie is hardly a booty call, but I can't let him even begin to suspect what's really going on. He'll sniff out the truth like a bloodhound. And then bite my head off.

Hayden shakes his head in mock disappointment. "Bros before hoes, dude. But I promise I won't be pissed...if you tell me who's been taking up all your free time."

"I don't have a new woman," I insist again, finger-combing my hair in quick, annoyed strokes. The guilty lie sits like something rotten in the bottom of my gut. "I've just been feeling tired."

"Okay, okay," he says, holding up his hands.

Keeping secrets from Hayden makes me feel like a complete asshole. He trusts me like a brother, and I'm lying to his face about fucking his sister. The whole situation is practically incest.

Maybe I should call things off with Gracie entirely. But the thought of never touching her again makes me feel so shitty. Even if we stayed friends afterward, it just wouldn't be the same. There would be a wall between us.

I discard the idea almost immediately. I can't help myself. I need to touch her again, at least one more time. Our secret rendezvous have to end soon anyway, so why not finish the job?

By the same token, saying, "I don't have a new woman" technically isn't even a lie. I don't *have* Gracie. Our arrangement is temporary. Two dates down, one to go—and then I have to set her free to live her own love life. With other men.

Gritting my teeth, I start tossing items in my gym bag, packing up to leave. But I pause when I pick up my phone and see that I have a text.

GRACIE: Hey sexy :P what are you doing tonight?

I glance up to check where Hayden is. He's finally gone to his locker and started getting dressed, so I type back a quick response before he can see my screen.

HUDSON: You, I hope. 8 at my place?

"I fucking knew it. Are you so pussy-whipped, you can't even wait to text her?"

My heart rate kicks up. I hit the power button to lock the screen just as Hayden tries to grab the phone out of my hand. "Look who's talking, dipshit," I fire back, trying not to sound as panicked as I feel. If he saw Gracie's name on that screen, or the text messages I've exchanged with her, he'd tear off my cock and feed it to me. Shoving him out of my personal space would help my mood, but it would also make him suspicious. "Emery's got you wrapped around her little finger."

"That's different. She's my girlfriend, not my fuck buddy."

"And we all know you're the world expert on how to treat women." I drop my phone back into my pocket. That was kind of a low blow, but in place of the angry frown I expected, Hayden huffs a little chuckle. I guess Emery really is changing him; he can laugh at the idiot he used to be.

As he heads for the locker room door, my phone buzzes. I pull it out, just for a second, and read Gracie's reply: *See you there. :)*

I was never doing these "lessons" just for Gracie's

benefit. But I never anticipated getting addicted to her so quickly. And now, no amount of guilt could ever outweigh my desire for her.

* * *

I go home to get ready for Gracie and kill time until she arrives. I take the wine out of the fridge and pour two glasses. I light a few candles, too, although I don't really know why—this isn't supposed to be romantic.

Gracie arrives ten minutes early, looking beautiful as always in a pink blouse and a pleated miniskirt that shows off her legs. It might be my imagination, but she seems even hotter than before we started sleeping together. More womanly, both mature and playful at the same time. She radiates confidence in her own sex appeal. Now she knows what she wants in the bedroom and she's comfortable enough to take it. Maybe I'm just on an ego trip here, but the thought that my instruction has helped her blossom...it feels pretty damn good.

Then the fact that this is our last evening together hits me. It'll be so hard to let her go after tonight. I can barely imagine never feeling her again. Never kissing her, pleasuring her...

Neither of us touch the wine I poured. We fall into each other, making out on the couch like a couple of teenagers, barely able to drag ourselves apart long enough to get to the bedroom. She seems just as hungry for me as I am for her. Wanting to make the most of our last night. Could she feel the same way I do?

But I push that thought to the back of my mind when she asks, "Will you teach me how to give a blowjob?"

I never thought I'd hear that word pass Gracie's lips. And she barely hesitated, too. I feel almost proud. I can't help but smirk. "We never did get around to that." It's always too easy to get caught up in ravishing her and forget about the original point of these lessons. I nod down at the tent in my jeans. "Take me out first."

She kneels down beside the bed and I spread my legs to make room for her. I hold myself still as she fumbles with the zipper and pulls out my cock, her eyes darkening with arousal. I groan quietly when she runs her thumb over the head, spreading precum over my most sensitive skin. Then she gives it an experimental lick, just to taste, and I shudder.

"Grip the base with one hand," I instruct. "No, tighter than that...remember what I said before. You're not going to break it."

She looks up at me. "I thought I was sucking it?" Her annoyed tone is adorable.

"You are, don't worry. You'll need to work the shaft with your hand while you concentrate on the top with your mouth. I'm going to tell you how to do it just right."

She looks back down at my cock, her gaze inquisitive, like she's plotting out a novel. Her fist only covers its bottom half. I can see the gears in her head turning, considering the best way to coordinate her efforts. I almost want to laugh; I've never seen anyone stare at me so thoughtfully, or approach a blowjob with so much planning. But that might embarrass her.

"Don't worry about trying to fit all of it in your mouth," I add. I'm about to tell her that I'll teach her how to deep-throat me another time, but then I remember there won't be another time. Before I'm able to dwell on that, Gracie runs her fist up and down my cock, reminding me to continue. "I want you to take me in your mouth—be careful of your teeth—and move your head up and down. When you get comfortable with that, try wiggling your tongue and sucking, too."

After another moment of assessment, Gracie goes for it. A long, low groan escapes me as she slides her mouth down over my cock. It's so warm, so soft, and I curse under my breath. Letting my hand rest on top of her head, I stroke her silky dark hair, and admire the way it shines almost gold where it catches the light.

It takes her a minute to figure out the rhythm, but soon, she's bobbing her head up and down after her hand like a champ. I wonder if she's been watching any pornos as research. Fuck, that's a hot mental image. Maybe I should pick out a good "educational" movie for us to watch next time. No, wait—there won't be a next time. Goddammit. Why can't I make that fact stick?

"D-don't try to show off by taking too much," I say, already starting to get a little unsteady. She's been a quick study so far, and this lesson is no exception. "No sense in gagging yourself."

Gracie makes a little indignant *hmph* noise that's way too cute for someone with a mouth full of dick. I feel her tongue slide over my flesh; she's impatient to prove herself, move on to the next step. And oh, *fuck*, she remembers that sensitive spot under the head...

The sounds of her wet slurps and my heavy breathing fill the room. Her cheeks hollow with suction. In a few minutes my balls start tightening up against my body, warm pleasure swirling through my veins. "I'm going to come soon," I warn her.

But instead of slowing down or stopping, she just hums loudly—where the hell did she learn that trick? My cock throbs at the vibration and I spurt into her mouth with a ragged groan. Her eyes widen, but she keeps sucking me off until I gasp, "Enough, baby." She immediately pulls off with a wet *pop*.

As I come down from my high, I can't help chuckling at the stricken look on her face. She swallows with visible effort and reaches for the nightstand to knock back a drink of water.

"*That's* what jizz tastes like?" she exclaims, mouth drawn down and nose wrinkled. "So...ugh."

Gracie fucking Oliver just drank down my come. *Damn.* "You're allowed to spit it out, you know. Or stop before I come." I pet her hair. "Did you like doing it at least?"

She considers it and then gives me a shy smile. "Yeah. I liked making you feel good. Knowing that I made you lose control turned me on."

Fuck...if she keeps talking like that, it won't take long before I'm hard again.

I help her up and back onto the bed. We lay on our sides and I pull her close, molding her body against mine, tasting myself in her kiss. I reach down—*Jesus, she's soaking wet*—and she gasps as my fingers slide over her swollen bud. I rub gently, enough to bring her closer to the edge but not nearly enough to push her over. I tease her clit until she's panting and rocking her hips into my hand, each breath edged with an urgent, keening note, and my cock is ready for action again.

I sit up, roll on a condom, and kneel between her legs. She wraps them around my waist, welcoming me. I slide in and her mouth opens in a soft moan, almost a hum of satisfaction. I'm suddenly very aware how big I am, and how small she looks under me. I'm almost a foot taller than her. She's so finely made, like a work of art. I know she's far from fragile. But though she's a spitfire sometimes, she's still soft and quiet deep down, and it shows when she's truly happy.

I draw my hips back and push in again, savoring the sight of that happiness spreading over her face. I vowed a long time ago that I would always protect Gracie. Make sure that life never hardened her all the way.

The very first children's book I'd left under her pillow was a fiftieth-anniversary edition of *Ferdinand the Bull*. When its stark red-and-black cover had caught my eye at the bookstore, I remembered the story I'd read in elementary school, which in turn reminded me of Gracie. Peaceful resistance—being true to herself, never getting mean or sour, but also never changing just for other people's sake. Even if that meant she felt out of place.

That afternoon, she ran down the stairs, her eyes lit up and cheeks glowing. Her family was getting ready to leave the house, their mom taking Hayden to some sports ceremony and their dad taking Beth to choir practice, leaving Gracie home alone again—I think she hated being alone, and she was left often. That's what drove me to do something special in the first place, something just for her. Anyway, she walked straight over to me and wrapped her fingers around my thumb, squeezing a gentle *thank you.*

Our careful dance continued from that moment on. Every few times I came over, she'd walk through the kitchen and briefly grab my thumb as she passed by, our hands concealed by the counter. It was innocent, but we both knew it was still borderline inappropriate. Hayden wouldn't have liked it. So, without ever explicitly agreeing on secrecy, we did it where no one could see.

Our own little moment, stolen here and there.

Well, Hayden sure as fuck wouldn't like this moment either. Me, rocking in and out of Gracie, spurring her cries of ecstasy louder and louder, feeling her body grasp me like she never wants to let go. Me, his best friend, slowly but surely...

Falling in love with his precious baby sister.

Her sapphire eyes blink up at mine, and worried she's going to see too much, I break our connection. "Turn over. On your hands and knees," I growl.

Chapter Nine

Gracie

"Right there, right there, don't stop," I pant, rocking back into his thrusts. Hudson moves with the surety of a man who knows exactly how to please a woman. I feel his thumb skim across my back opening and he growls out a curse.

Tonight we've gotten more inventive with new positions and I'm amazed at how different it can feel— so, so deep when I rode him, and now with him behind me again, I feel incredibly full.

Hudson's fingers dig into my hips as he pulls me back on his cock. I can feel him thicken inside me and I know he's close. It only fuels my own desire for release. I want to be right there with him.

I reach between my legs and begin to rub my clit, very much wanting to join him in the fun. He pushes my hand away and begins using his own to massage me in tight circles. "That's my job," he whispers, leaning forward to plant a kiss between my shoulder blades. "You just concentrate on coming, baby."

It's so incredibly sexy how completely he takes ownership of my body. With that thought, I begin rocking back against him faster. His fingers are still moving over my clit, but his other hand is planted on the bed beside mine. I reach over, wrap my fingers around his large thumb and squeeze. Our secret language from so long ago that I'm sure he's forgotten by now. But it soothes me, helps feed the craving in my heart. Makes me feel even more connected to him.

"Baby, you look so sexy riding my dick like this." His voice is strained, and I let go, bucking wildly into his hips and coming harder than I ever have in my life.

"Fuuuuck," Hudson growls behind me, pumping into me in deep, uneven thrusts as he comes right along with me.

All of my muscles are trembling as he carefully lifts me up, pulling me close to his chest. Even if I wanted to, I couldn't support my body weight right now; I'm thankful to be folded into his strong arms.

As fantastic as the sex is between us, I think the after-part is my favorite. This cozy peace. When he holds me tight and our hearts gallop together until finally our breathing slows. Sometimes we make small conversation, and sometimes we're just quiet—in the moment together.

But tonight, as I lay here in his arms, a sinking feeling grows in the pit of my stomach.

I feel a lot more for him than I should, and now this is it. The end of the road for us. What was I thinking? Despite Melanie's warning, despite my own constant scolding, I hadn't been protecting my heart. I only meant to give him my body, but somehow, he took all of me. And I don't know what I could have done to stop it.

Blinking back tears, I climb out of his bed and pad barefoot into the bathroom.

After splashing cool water onto my cheeks, I look up at my reflection. The apples of my cheeks are flushed and my hair's a disaster. I look like I've been thoroughly fucked. And that's exactly it. I'm fucked. I'm falling in love with a man I can never have. A single tear slips from my eye and rolls slowly down my cheek as I stare in the mirror, like I'm watching someone else's heart break.

"Gracie?" Hudson calls from outside the door.

"Just a minute," I say, relieved that my voice sounds calm. Wiping away the tears, I gulp down a deep lungful of air and unlock the door.

As I stride past him, he chuckles and grabs me around the waist. "Where do you think you're going?"

I stop and spin to face him. He must see something in my expression, because all the humor in his face fades. "What's wrong?"

My lower lip trembles. "Nothing. I need to go home, that's all. I mean, we're done, right? Three times. You took my virginity."

A crease appears between his brows. "Hey, I didn't *take* anything. We shared this. And it was fantastic." He places his hands on my shoulders and gives them a squeeze. His pep talk reminds me of a coach preparing a down-and-out player to return to the big game. But this was never a game to me, and I can never go back. Not to his bed, not to the warm safety of his arms. I feel shattered and hollow. And so incredibly alone.

"Right. And now we're done." My voice is cold and emotionless. But it needs to be. I hadn't been protecting myself before, but that changes starting now.

"Are you okay?" he asks, his tone softening as he watches me.

This whole situation is made all the more awkward by the fact that we're both still naked. His soft cock hanging between us is a sad reminder that everything's over now.

"I'm fine," I say, crossing the room and stepping into my underwear as a stray tear escapes. *Damn it.* Trying not to let him see, I wipe it away with the back of my hand.

"You're not fine." He takes my hand and leads me back to his bed, which looks like a bomb went off in it. The blankets are scattered everywhere and the sheets are tangled. The pillows got kicked to the floor over an hour ago. We sit down on the end of the bed and I stare down at the floor between my feet. "Please tell me what you're thinking," he presses gently. "Do you regret this?"

I want to tell him no, but the truth is, part of me does. If I knew how absolutely miserable I'd feel after it ended, I don't know if I would have agreed to this. When I registered on those dating sites, it wasn't just to lose my virginity; it was to find someone I could date, maybe even see a future with. But Hudson isn't that person. I should have kept that in mind from the beginning. "I'm not sure," I start. "I mean, for you to be my first … it's what I'd always wanted. But now that it's over, it just kind of … sucks."

He doesn't say anything, but when I glance over at him, his jaw is set firm and I can see his pulse pumping in his neck. I have no idea what he's thinking. *Crap, I said way too much.* I just admitted I've always wanted to fuck him. *Great…now he's going to think I'm obsessed with him. Not that that's far from the truth.*

I open my mouth to tell him never mind, I'm just going to go home. But instead I start rambling like I always do when I'm nervous. "When you suggested these three lessons, I was so happy, but now I'm feeling sad that it's over, and I'm sorry because I know you don't do relationships."

He exhales slowly, audibly, in the otherwise silent room.

I'm sure he's about to shoot me down, tell me all the reasons why we can't be together. My brother would never allow it, or I'm too young for him, or he might just agree with me that he's not looking for a relationship.

But instead of doing any of that, he rises to his feet and begins pacing across his bedroom.

Then he stops abruptly and looks down, seeming to realize that he's still naked.

He grabs his boxer briefs and puts them on. "This is too important of a conversation to have naked." He smirks at me.

"S-should I get dressed?" I ask.

Shaking his head, he steps close. "No, you're perfect the way you are."

He stands directly in front of me and lifts my chin, holding my cheek in his large palm while his thumb skims along my skin. I take a deep breath, preparing myself for the sting of his words. I'm sure he'll try to let me down easy, but it still feels …

"You're right. I don't do relationships. I've never found the appeal. But these past few nights with you have been incredible. So even though I don't know what I'm doing when it comes to relationships…I've always wanted you too. And now that we've started this, the last thing I want to do is stop."

I blink my eyes, sure I just imagined what I heard. "What are you saying?" A few hopeful butterflies are already waking up in my stomach.

"I'm saying, let's do this. We owe it to ourselves to at least try and see where this goes. We have a great time together. In bed and out of it. And I'm sure as fuck not ready to let you walk away and date one of these dickheads from that website."

I giggle, delirious happiness bubbling up inside me. Until my thoughts drift to my brother. "What about Hayden?" I frown, chewing on my lip.

"You let me deal with that."

Somehow the knot of worry in my stomach eases. I have no idea what will happen next, but I trust Hudson. I always have. And if he says he can take care of it— take care of me—then I believe him.

I fall into his arms and we share sweet, tender kisses and even sweeter words. My thoughts still darken whenever I think about what my brother's reaction to all of this will be. But Hudson is here for me. Whatever the future holds, he's on my side.

"You want to try Sebastian's again?" Hudson asks, placing a kiss on my forehead.

I chuckle. "I'm not ten anymore … we don't have to go for ice cream."

"I know. But our last date got cut short. And I want to take you out...in public. With me. Hold your hand and feed you bites of dessert."

"What if we see Hayden again? Are you going to disappear on me?" There's a worried note to my voice, no matter how cool I'm trying to play this new relationship thing we're navigating.

He sits up, pulling me up with him. "I'm not going anywhere."

If Hayden saw us out together, reeking of sex, he'd punch Hudson in the face. Not that Hudson couldn't defend himself, but still, it's not a scenario I care to dwell on. But I see in his expression that Hudson's set on this idea. Maybe he just wants a do-over, to paint some good memories over the awkward one from a few days ago.

"Can I borrow a T-shirt?" I ask.

"Of course you can."

Thirty minutes later, we're once again standing in line for ice cream cones. But the atmosphere couldn't be more different than last time. Hudson holds my hand the entire time we're in line, and when he leans down to place soft kisses against the back of my neck, murmuring that he loves seeing me in his T-shirt, I almost melt into a puddle. Our date is happy instead of bittersweet, openly affectionate instead of secretive. The future is all spread out for us to choose from, like the ice cream flavors in their big inviting tubs, every option bright and sweet. Everything this transition means—leaving the bedroom and acting like a couple in public—is nothing short of a dream come true.

Epilogue

Hudson

One Year Later

"Stand still," Hayden mutters. "Your bow tie is more crooked than a dog's hind leg."

I laugh, jostling his hands even more. "And you're picking up some seriously hokey shit from Emery's mom."

He grins. "What can I say? Her Midwest-isms are catchy." He finishes adjusting my tie and slaps me on the shoulder. "I still can't believe you're getting married, dude. And before me, too. How the fuck did that happen?"

I know what he means. If someone had told me last year that I'd find a girlfriend by now—let alone a wife—I would have laughed in their face. And then probably punched them. I didn't understand why or how a man could tie himself down like that.

But Gracie showed me that a good relationship doesn't tie you down. It sets you free. It means that you'll always have someone there to support you. It gives you a space to be yourself without being alone. To try new things together and fuck up and laugh about it and try again.

Ever since we were kids, I'd always had feelings for Gracie. But I didn't understand just how deep they ran. And when I started to realize it, I instinctively fought the idea. Love was a drug, a trap, a trick that only other people fell for. My being in love with Gracie would change everything. I'd have to give up my playboy lifestyle, Hayden wouldn't trust me anymore, and Gracie's heart would probably end up broken.

But it was already too late. From the moment we first kissed, her tongue eagerly stroking mine in that crowded nightclub hallway, I had started changing...for the better.

Then, on the night of our last *lesson*, I couldn't deny the truth any longer. Seeing Gracie cry over me had felt like a gut-punch. *I know you don't do relationships*, she said, and instead of nodding along, I realized something: I genuinely wanted one. I wanted to try. I wanted to learn. So I let her know that it was her turn to become my teacher. And she did. She showed me how to love—in her own way, full of laughter, passion, and heat. I never knew something could feel so all encompassing. She was my first thought when I woke up and the last thing on my mind when I drifted off to sleep. It was her name on my lips when we made love, her very being imprinted on my heart. It was love with no guardrails, and I fell hard and deep for her.

Now I'm standing in a cramped church dressing room, wearing a tuxedo, ready to make an honest woman out of her. With my closest friend by my side.

That last part still feels crazy to me sometimes, even though it's been almost a year since I manned up and came clean with Hayden. I told him I wanted to date his kid sister—real, serious dates, not just hands-on sex ed. That dinner was one of the most awkward things I've ever sat through. But somehow, instead of the train wreck I'd expected, it was only a minor speed bump in our friendship. And two hours after I proposed to her, Hayden had called me to demand why I hadn't asked him to be my best man yet.

Maybe it worked out because he saw how crazy I am about Gracie. My feelings were so obvious that Hayden knew deep down, that I could never hurt her. He saw it in my eyes and he heard it in my voice, so rather than punch me in the face, like I was expecting, he sat there and listened to my every word.

"You guys are still getting dressed?" Beth pokes her head in, looking frazzled but proud. No force on Earth could have kept her from being Gracie's matron of honor. "It's showtime. Get your asses out there."

We both swear and hurry down the back hallway to the main chapel. We reach the altar just minutes before the organ belts out its first notes. A wave of nerves hits me, but they're the good kind of jitters. I can't wait to see Gracie today.

All the guests coo as the flower girl and ring bearer appear: Beth's two preschoolers, Georgia and Austin, looking like dolls in their fancy miniature clothes. They're only four and five years old, so it's a minor miracle when they make it down the aisle without a hitch. Beth bends down, smiling and holding out her hands in encouragement, until they reach the

125 • *Monster Prick | Kendall Ryan*

bridesmaids' section and the safety of their mother's arms. Georgia offers a daisy to Melanie, causing another wave of *aww*'s to sweep through the pews.

Then the music holds its breath, Gracie walks through the chapel doors...and I can't see a damn thing but her anymore. As I watch my stunning bride draw closer, every emotion crashes into me at once. She looks like an angel. With her gown's elegant, floor-length skirt, she even seems to float forward on a cloud rather than walk. Her lush chestnut hair spills over her shoulders in a riot of curling waves, natural and not done-up like I was expecting. Her cheeks and lips have been stained the same girlish, kissable pink. Her V-shaped neckline hangs low from wide, see-through straps; I want to bite her delicate exposed collarbones, push my face into the cleavage that just barely peeks out. Damn, I never thought a wedding gown could be sexy as well as beautiful. But I guess that's because the woman inside it is Gracie.

Her eyes latch onto mine as she draws closer, and she gives me a cheeky smile. She doesn't look nervous or unsure, just ridiculously happy, and I thank my lucky stars she's mine. All of her. Heart, body, and soul. And seeing her in a white dress right now? It's pretty fucking surreal.

She'd look even better *out* of the dress, but I'll get to see that treat soon enough. My imagination drifts ahead to our honeymoon. In less than six hours, we'll be kicking back at a luxury resort hotel in Puerto Vallarta. I can sip a margarita on my beach chair and watch Gracie frolic in a skimpy bikini, the lapping ocean waves as blue as her eyes. And after the sun sets...

I'm especially looking forward to our wedding night. Not because we'll do anything new in bed—it would be hard to find a box we haven't checked yet, at least not without getting into some seriously crazy shit—but because we ourselves will be new people. We'll be making love as husband and wife for the first time. A virginity we'll lose together.

As the music fades to a close, Gracie steps up onto the altar, across the pulpit from me. I lean over to pull her near before the music dies entirely and the minister starts talking. "You still sure about this?" I whisper into her ear. "No backing out now."

She blinks, half-smiling, as if she's not sure whether I'm joking or she just misheard me. "I'm not going anywhere."

"Good. Because you're about to become mine forever."

Her half-smile spreads into that beaming grin I love to see, dimples and all. "There's nothing I want more," she murmurs.

My heart skips a beat. The minister clears his throat and I step back into place, my gaze still locked with Gracie's, ready to begin our new life.

Acknowledgments

Thank you so much to the readers who supported *Screwed* – my first attempt at a romantic comedy. I had a blast writing it, and was blown away by your warm reception for Hayden and Emery's love story. I didn't anticipate writing *Monster Prick*, but sometimes the characters decide for you, just as Hudson and Gracie did here. Despite having written more than twenty books, I'd never written a novella before. It made me a little nervous! But it turned out just adorable and I hope you enjoyed the story as much as I did.

A big thank you to Danielle Sanchez, Angela Smith, and Rachel Brookes. You each play a significant role in helping me on my writing journey. Each novel is different, some more difficult than others, so thank you for being there to support me.

To all of the bloggers, fans, and readers who have shared my books with others, who've left reviews and made beautiful graphic teasers, my heart is filled with bookish love for you. I hope you know how critical you are to this community. I'm grateful for every tweet, review, and mention. My readers mean everything to me, and I'm blessed to have your support.

To my little family. You're everything to me.

About the Author

A *New York Times*, *Wall Street Journal*, and *USA Today* bestselling author of more than a dozen titles, Kendall Ryan has sold more than a million ebooks and her books have been translated into several languages in countries around the world. She's a traditionally published author with Simon & Schuster and Harper Collins UK, as well as an independently published author. Since she first began self-publishing in 2012, she's appeared at #1 on Barnes & Noble and iBooks charts around the world. Her books have also appeared on the New York Times and USA Today bestseller list more than two dozen times. Ryan has been featured in such publications as USA Today, Newsweek, and InTouch Weekly.

Visit her website for more: www.kendallryanbooks.com

Coming Soon

Bait & Switch, Alphas Undone Book 1

Love is a trap, a trick only other people fall for. Former Navy SEAL Nolan has no such illusions. The only things real in his life are his beloved bulldog and the two women who regularly share his bed. One is light—soft, innocent, and tender touches. The other is dark—and gives him all of the wicked things he craves behind closed doors. It's not cheating when each is aware of the other. But when he begins to feel much more than he ever bargained for, the order of his carefully crafted world is shaken, and he stands to lose everything.

Nolan thinks we met by chance. We didn't. I sought him out, seduced him, and in return got the sanctuary I needed to survive. But now, impossibly, I've fallen in love with him. I don't care that he has another lover, because when he finds out who I am, it's going to ruin any chance I ever had with him anyway. She's the least of my worries.

Bait & Switch is Book 1 in a new contemporary romance series by Kendall Ryan. It will be released on February 9, 2016.

Other Books by Kendall Ryan

UNRAVEL ME Series:

Unravel Me

Make Me Yours

LOVE BY DESIGN Series:

Working It

Craving Him

All or Nothing

WHEN I BREAK Series:

When I Break

When I Surrender

When We Fall

FILTHY BEAUTIFUL LIES Series:

Filthy Beautiful Lies

Filthy Beautiful Love

Filthy Beautiful Lust

Filthy Beautiful Forever

LESSONS WITH THE DOM Series:

The Gentleman Mentor

Sinfully Mine

STAND-ALONE NOVELS:

Hard to Love

Reckless Love

Resisting Her

The Impact of You

Screwed

Made in the USA
San Bernardino, CA
14 November 2015